The Mwindo Epic
from the Banyanga

The Mwindo Epic
from the Banyanga

―――

Edited and translated by

Daniel Biebuyck

and

Kahombo C. Mateene

UNIVERSITY OF CALIFORNIA PRESS

University of California Press, one of the most distinguished university presses in the United States, enriches lives around the world by advancing scholarship in the humanities, social sciences, and natural sciences. Its activities are supported by the UC Press Foundation and by philanthropic contributions from individuals and institutions. For more information, visit www.ucpress.edu.

University of California Press
Oakland, California

ISBN 978-0-520-37980-0 (pbk.: alkaline paper)
ISBN 978-0-520-38463-7 (ebook)

Library of Congress Catalog Card Number: 68-28370

Manufactured in the United States of America

30 29 28 27 26 25 24 23 22 21
10 9 8 7 6 5 4 3 2 1

In April, 1956, I organized a field expedition of several weeks into one of the most remote forest areas of Nyanga country, an area then known as *groupement Kisimba* in Belgian administrative circles. I had been actively engaged in field research among the Nyanga since April, 1954. The Nyanga had known me since late 1952 when, working among the Bembe and the Lega, I had on several occasions visited them in order to plan for future research projects.

By the time of my trip to Kisimba, I had acquired a broad knowledge of Nyanga culture, I had a good grasp of the language, I was well accepted by the people, I knew all the key informants, and I had been able to recruit an excellent team of collaborators. These included two categories of people: on the one hand, Mr. Amato Buuni and Mr. Stephano Tubi, two young men born and raised in the Nyanga milieu, who had finished their junior high school studies and whom I had trained in field methods since late 1952; on the other hand, two older Nyanga, Sherungu and Kanyangara, who had not been to school, but who possessed an admirable knowledge of Nyanga culture and who held important ritual and political offices in the Nyanga political system. Whereas Mr. Buuni and Mr. Tubi acted as clerks, writing down texts and various types of supplementary information, Mr. Sherungu and Mr. Kanyangara were readily available, first-class informants and *hommes de confiance* who could critically advise me on data obtained from my other informants in the various villages.

By the time I was planning my Kisimba trip, I had already visited large sections of Nyanga country, making routine ethnological investigations and writing down, with the help of Mr. Buuni and Mr. Tubi, hundreds of tales, narratives of events and dreams, and thousands of proverbs, riddles, songs, prayers, incantations, and praise formulas. I knew for a long time that the Nyanga had a longer, more expanded type of story, classified by them under the special name *kárj̧sj̧*. On a couple of occasions I had received fragments of such stories from select informants, but I had never been successful in getting a complete and coherent text, either because the narrator was too old and too confused or because he did not remember the complete text (or had never known it), or because the narrator was simply uncooperative and apprehensive of the necessity to sit day after day with me and my collaborators to painstakingly narrate—indeed narrate over and over again—the various passages of his *kárj̧sj̧*-story.

Then, on my Kisimba trip, while doing the routine work of taking village censuses, writing down genealogies, collecting information on descent groups, on kinship patterns, on political structure, on religion, and the like, I met Mr. Shé-kárj̧sj̧ Rureke in the village of Bese. Very cooperative and understanding, very lucid and intelligent, Rureke sat down with us for twelve days, singing, narrating, dancing, miming, until the present text was completely written down.

These days represent a great and memorable time in my life, one of the the highlights of my long fieldwork in Zaire. We would begin to work early in the morning and, with a few short breaks, continue well into the night. Large crowds of people from Bese and from surrounding villages and hamlets would come to listen to the narration, to participate in the refrains of the songs, to dance. There was an atmosphere of joy and relaxation in this village where, as in the other Nyanga villages, life had become increasingly dull and joyless as a result of the various pressures introduced from the outside.

Rureke himself was inexhaustible in words, in movements, in rhythm, even though he became very tired physically (during the last days, his voice became increasingly hoarse and I was compelled to treat him regularly with some European ointments and mouthwashes). Very excited by the stimulus he received from his audience, very self-confident about his knowledge, and very proud about his achievements, Rureke was able to maintain from beginning to end the coherence of his story and the unusual richness and precision of language, as well as to capture the essence of Nyanga values.

Because of a variety of other duties and commitments, this great narrative has remained hidden in my files for a long period. In 1956 and 1958, I published in Dutch translation small fragments of it in a periodical, *Zuiderkruis*, which was published in Léopoldville. In 1964, thanks to a generous grant from the Alumni Foundation of the University of Delaware, I was able to bring to the United States one of my former students in Léopoldville, Mr. Kahombo C. Mateene, Nyanga by birth, trained in African linguistics and anthropology at the universities of Lovanium (Zaire), Delaware, and California (Los Angeles). In close collaboration, we have worked on the definite establishment of the Nyanga text, on the translation, and on the notes.

I am pleased to present here, as the fruit of long and painstaking travail, this Mwindo epic in the Bantu text and in English translation. This epic is certainly a tribute to the rich content of Nyanga culture and to the creative talent of Mr. Rureke and his predecessors.

My sincere thanks go to my Nyanga informants and collaborators, particularly to the narrator himself, Mr. Shé-kárjsj Rureke, for their loyal assistance in helping me to save from oblivion part of so great a cultural tradition. I want to express my appreciation for the unfaltering encouragement and sponsorship I received during my fieldwork in Zaire from the Belgian Research Institute, Institut pour la recherche scientifique en Afrique centrale, and, in particular, from its former secretary-general, Dr. Jean-Paul Harroy, and its former director-general, Dr. Louis van den Berghe. The University of Delaware and the African Studies Center of the University of California, Los Angeles, have kindly provided me with the grants necessary for permitting Mr. Kahombo C. Mateene to work with me on this project. Finally, I want to acknowledge the dedicated work done by Mrs. Lorraine Przywara in Delaware and Miss Andrée Slaughter in California in the typing of the manuscript and in the improving and correcting of the English text.

In the field, the epic text was recorded in writing (with tonal indication) jointly by Amato Buuni, Stephano Tubi, and myself. The preface, introduction, and notes in their present form are entirely my responsibility. The definite establishment of the Nyanga text and the method of word division are the work of Mr. Mateene. The translation is the result of intensive collaboration by Kahombo C. Mateene, Amato Buuni, Stephano Tubi, and myself.

D. B.

CONTENTS

Miréngé esímbănge băte

Ná barįmį bátásibéyo.

The tunes [voices] that we sing

The uninitiated ones [the ignorant ones] cannot understand them.

—FROM THE MWINDO EPIC

Introduction

THE NYANGA[1]

The 27,000 Bantu-speaking Nyanga live in the mountainous rain forest area of Walikale territory in the former Kivu Province, in the eastern part of Zaire, Kinshasa. The ethnohistorical traditions are weakly developed and are primarily concerned with the establishment and distribution of the Nyanga in their present habitat. All these traditions, however, point to origins in East Africa and more particularly in Bunyoro and Toro (Uganda). Migrating from East Africa, the Nyanga settled for some time in the grasslands and on the mountain slopes on the Zaire side of the Lake Edward region, where several remnant

---

1. For further general information on the Nyanga see the following studies by D. Biebuyck: "De mumbo-instelling by de Banyanga (Kivu)," *Kongo Overzee*, XXI (1955), 441–448; *De Hond by de Nyanga: Ritueel en Sociologie* (Brussels: Académie royale des Sciences d'Outre-Mer, 1956), 168 pp.; "L'organisation politique des Nyanga: La chefferie Ihana," *Kongo Overzee*, XXII (1956), 301–341; XXIII (1957), 59–98; "Mwéndo de Zwoeger: Een heldedicht van de Banyanga," *Zuiderkruis*, I (1956), 77–80; III (1958), 35–45; "Les divisions du jour et de la nuit chez les Nyanga," *Aequatoria*, XXI (1958), 134–138; "Six Nyanga Texts," in W. H. Whiteley, ed., *A Selection of African Prose* (Oxford: Clarendon Press, 1964), I, 55–61; "Prières des chasseurs Nyanga," in G. Dieterlen, ed., *Textes sacrés d'Afrique noire* (Paris: Gallimard, 1965), pp. 135–143; *Rights in Land and Its Resources among the Nyanga* (Brussels: Académie royale des Sciences d'Outre-Mer, 1966). A broad selection of Nyanga texts is ready now and will be published in 1967 under the title *Anthologie de la littérature orale nyanga* by the Académie royale des Sciences d'Outre-Mer, Brussels.

1

groups of this migration are found today. Moving southwestward from there, the Nyanga gradually infiltrated the rain forest. Nyanga oral traditions explicitly state that in the rain forest their forefathers met with small, scattered groups of at least three different ethnic units: Pygmies, called Twa or more specifically Remba; Tiro-Asa of Kumu origin; Mpamba of Lega affiliation. Smaller remnants of Pygmies and Lega, and larger groups of Tiri-Asa (Kumu), are still found in Nyanga country. All are culturally closely interwoven with the Nyanga. Among them, the biologically miscegenated groups identified as Pygmies play a most significant role. They are attached by strong political and ritual bonds to the Nyanga sacred chiefs: they are the chief's hunters, they hold various ritual offices connected with the chief's enthronement, they provide the chief with one of his ritual wives (whose firstborn son holds the ritual position of *mwǎmítwá*, lit., chief Pygmy), and they are traditionally the chief's bards, experts in narrating and singing the longer epic tales. To the entire Nyanga population, they stand in some sort of joking relationship in that, for example, they are allowed to freely harvest plantains in all banana groves.

The impact of Pygmy culture on the Nyanga has been very strong. This is visible, for example, in some of the techniques and beliefs associated with hunting and food-gathering, and in the cult system, where the Nyanga worship, among other divinities, Měshémutwá (Meshe the Pygmy). The Nyanga assertion that their great epic texts, like the one presented here, originally flourished with those Nyanga groups that were most intimately associated with the Pygmies, contains an important culture-historical reference and points to the possibility that these epics or at least their basic themes originated with the Pygmies. I did not, however, find any special awareness of this fact among the so-called Pygmies whom I met in this region between 1956 and 1958.

Above all, the Nyanga are trappers, food-gatherers, and cultivators, but they also hunt and fish. Nyanga economy and diet are based on the complementary relationship among these various activities, which may receive different degrees of emphasis owing to limited local specialization. Dive-fishing, for example, or big-game hunting by highly esoteric corporations of hunters is found only in certain select Nyanga villages. As is revealed in rituals, taboos, legal principles of distribution and sharing, principles of land tenure, and as is also clear from the events and values suggested in hundreds of tales, trapping is the single most significant economic activity in Nyanga society. Agriculture is centered on the growing of the plantain banana. The system of cultivation is very extensive and informal and is based on the "slash without burning technique." Over the years, new banana groves are added to the existing ones in a cyclic shifting pattern; the banana groves, nevertheless, yield for many years, the duration of productivity depending upon the degree of maintenance. The Nyanga also traditionally cultivate a variety of grain and root crops, which are planted either in or on the edge of the banana grove. The sowing or planting of some subsidiary crops requires the partial burning of grasses and branches accumulated in patches of the banana grove.

The ideology of descent, inheritance, and succession is patrilineal, The descent groups themselves are thought to be patrilineal and are built around a nucleus of *de facto* or *de jure* agnatically related kinsmen. But membership in these patrilineally focused descent groups is not determined merely by unilineal male kinship bonds. In order to understand this feature of the Nyanga social structure, it is necessary to distinguish between two basic types of marriage. First is the more classic form of marriage based on the transfer in stages from the man's group to the wife's group of a fixed number of matrimonial goods which establishes for the husband and father the right to affiliate children born of that marriage with his own descent group. Second are the marriages between women and spirits, which are decided upon by the agnatic relatives of the women as a result of dreams, oracles, and so on. These spirit wives are permitted to live in what are usually prolonged, stable unions with married or unmarried "lovers" of either their own or their agnates' choice. These "lovers" have sexual rights to and various domestic and economic claims on the women, but cannot legally affiliate with their own descent groups the children born of these unions. In other words, spirit wives—who are found in large numbers throughout Nyanga society, in all descent groups—procreate children in the name of the agnatic descent groups of their fathers, brothers, and paternal uncles. In the course of time these uterine relatives are identified in genealogical recitations, as well as in the actual kinship nomenclature, with the male agnatic nucleus of the descent groups of their mothers; that is, they are treated as descendants of their unmarried mother's brothers.

Some descent groups are named after a male eponymous founder, others are known by nicknames and epithets. The known genealogical charts are shallow in depth and subject to considerable manipulation. The descent groups themselves are dispersed units consisting of several small localized corporate units composed of one or several agnatically related extended families. Each of the descent groups has a core area or a cradle area with which, before the colonial policy of resettlement was introduced, at least one of its localized family units is associated as *miné* (owner, lord, legally and mystically linked with . . .).

Politically the Nyanga are organized into autonomous petty states, each ruled by a sacred chief (*mwǎmí*). The chiefs are recruited in only a limited number of descent groups, some of which are considered to be agnatically related to one another, a practice that makes provision for special bonds of cooperation or at least of friendship among several autonomous chiefs. The sacred chiefs, surrounded by nobles (*barúsi̧*), counselors (*bakungú*), and ritual officeholders (*bandírabitambo*), have directly under their control the different village headmen whose villages lie within the limits of the state. In other words, each petty state is territorially subdivided into a number of villages and hamlets; there exists no other intermediate territorial grouping.

Ancestral cult is little developed among the Nyanga: people occasionally pray to a dead agnatic relative (father, paternal grandfather, or paternal aunt) but there are no shrines nor is there an intensive worship of the ancestors. The entire cult system is built around a number of divinities, most of whom, like Muisa, Kiana, Hángi̧, Meshe, Nkángo, Kahómbó, are said to live together with the dead in the Underworld (*kwirúngá*, a place identified with the craters of the active and extinct volcanoes that are found east of Nyanga country, on the boundaries of Zaire and Rwanda) under the leadership of Nyamurairi̧, god of fire.

Some other divinities which are actively worshiped, such as Kéntsé (Sun), Nkúbá (Lightning), Iyúhu (Wind), Kibira (Leopard), Musóka (Water Serpent), are said to have left the Underworld to live in the sky, on earth, or in the water. All these divinities, together with the ancestors, are known under the generic term *bashumbú*. Shrines are made and plantains are grown for them, women are dedicated and married to them, sheep and hunting dogs are consecrated to them, prayers are said to them, and distinctive cultual paraphernalia for each of them are kept by their adepts. They manifest themselves in dreams and oracles and are responsible for good and evil in Nyanga life. The earth is further peopled with the land-dwelling dragon Kiri̧mu, the forest specter Mpacá, and the Binyanyasi̧ (restless spirits of those Nyanga who committed suicide or died, stigmatized as sorcerers, as the result of a *kabi̧*-ordeal), and by the water-dwelling, rather friendly monster Muki̧ti̧. The Nyanga formulate several ideas about Ongo, God, who is said *inter alia* to be the "heart of the earth," to have created everything, to be the giver of life (*buingo*), to have given man the knowledge that he possesses. Finally, the Nyanga have elaborate boys' circumcision rites. They also possess a wide variety of semisecret associations (membership in which is mostly restricted to certain descent groups) none of which has a tribe-wide adherence or distribution.

The profusion of Nyanga oral literature stands in contrast to the fairly limited, though highly efficient, technology. The Nyanga possess an impressive variety of fishing, trapping, and hunting devices, but the wickerwork, plaiting, ironwork, pottery, and carving are simple. Wooden dishes and pots are decorated with incised designs. Plastic art is practically unknown in world collections, although the Nyanga make decorative masks of antelope hide, a rare type of anthropo-zoomorphic wooden statue used in the *mumbírá*-initiations and very rare bone and ivory carvings for the *mbúntsú* association.

NYANGA ORAL LITERATURE

The small Nyanga tribe possesses a highly diversified oral literature, rich in content and style. There are innumerable situations and occurrences that occasion the recitation, singing, or narration of the traditional texts. The Nyanga live in an isolated and largely undisturbed environment where social relationships among individuals, families, and larger groups of kinsmen are intensive and intimate. Daily, after returning from work in the forest, small groups of men—agnates, affines, friends—sit together in the men's meeting place to eat, drink, smoke, discuss the day's events, assign the next day's tasks, analyze patterns of behavior and action, scrutinize personal and familial problems, instruct the children in the social mores, criticize misconduct. These routine gatherings, which often extend long into the night, are a major occasion for narrating tales, quoting proverbs, solving riddles, not merely as a form of entertainment and fun, but also as a means of clarification of ideas, of interpretation of events, and of enhancement of existing values.

In their own domestic sphere, the women of the village also gather, in small groups of three or four in the company of their younger children, to eat, chat, and instruct. Like the men, they narrate stories, recite proverbs, and solve riddles, which, though similar in content and theme to those of the men, are commonly different in conclusion or explanation. Adolescents, too, males and females living in their own spheres, daily participate in dances for sheer entertainment or in games, an intrinsic part of which are traditional songs, riddles, proverbs. In addition to these regular daily activities, there are the hundreds of special occasions—rites, initiations, statewide councils, specialized dances—which are inconceivable without narrated, sung, recited texts, oral texts that either belong to the common patrimony or are the possessions of specialized groups and specific categories of people.

All Nyanga know a certain number of texts; some are able to narrate, sing, or recite them coherently and completely, others are confused narrators, able only to communicate the essence of their content. The expert narrators or singers do not make a profession of or derive a special social status from their skill. They may be in demand and thus receive much food, banana beer, and small presents. They may be famed and praised for their art, but they are not looked upon as a group of specialists, nor can they make a living of it. The expert narrators and singers may know a fairly large number of texts, but rarely does their knowledge approach the unusually high level and competence of that of Mr. Sherungu Muriro, one of the great Nyanga informants, who gave me 21 very long tales, 82 "true" stories, 43 interpretations of dreams, 268 riddles, 327 songs (some mere proverbs, others long and complex concatenations of aphorisms and personal reflections and remembrances).

The Nyanga musical instruments, inseparable from the dances, initiations, and gatherings of which the oral literature is an integral part, cover the following range. There are three types of funnel-shaped drums of different sizes (ioma, mukíntsa, kandúndú, beaten with two hands, two drumsticks, one drumstick, respectively); the percussion stick (nkwángátiro); the antelope horn (kahanda); the small reed or bamboo flute (kaféréré); the calabash or wickerwork rattle (ịshengo); the music bow (kimpúrenge); the two-stringed zither (ntsentse); the three types of zanzas (kantsambi, ikímbi, and kasáị, the last of recent introduction); the anklet bells (ntsumbo) made from nutshells or iron.

Any type of text, except prayers, can be narrated, recited, and/or sung with the accompaniment of some of these musical instruments or of simple handclapping, but certain dances, initiations, or narratives require specific instruments or combinations of instruments. Praise songs for chiefs, headmen, and mountains, for example, may be accompanied by only two rattles, two drums, and the small flute.

We have prepared for publication an anthology of Nyanga oral literature[2] in which selected samples of the various forms of this literature are given. A brief description of these forms as they are classified by the Nyanga follows.

mushúmo. This category comprises proverbs, maxims, and other terse statements that represent part of the Nyanga code of values. Almost all teachings and precepts given in the course of initiations are presented in the form of proverbs that are sung or recited. Most of the so-called songs (*rwimbo*) consist of nothing but concatenations of proverbs intermingled with reflections improvised by the singer. In legal contexts and in a very wide range of discussions and arguments, proverbs are currently quoted. All Nyanga proverbs are to be thought of as a form of poetry. The majority of them are composed of two verses, separated by a caesura. Quite often, the Nyanga reciter formulates only the first verse, leaving the task of either thinking or actually phrasing the second one to his audience. The structure of these verses follows definite quantitative patterns (e.g., number of words and syllables) as well as qualitative patterns (e.g., rhyme, alliteration, assonance, reduplication). Frequently, the normal tone pattern is changed to enhance the qualities of rhythm. Both men and women know proverbs, but men make the most extensive use of them.

inondo. These are riddles that are most commonly used by adolescents and women. More restricted in their range of applicability, the riddles are less rich in content than the proverbs. They are sung or recited and accompanied by handclapping, gestures, rhythmic movements. Like the proverbs, most Nyanga riddles are a form of poetry consisting of two verses. The first verse contains a statement, a proposition, a compound personal name, rarely a purely onomatopoeic form, and may or may not be introduced by a verbal expression

2. To be published in 1968 in the *Collections* of the Académie royale des Sciences d'Outre-Mer, Brussels.

meaning "Tell me," "Teach me," "May I know," or "Beware." The second verse provides the answer, which may be a single word, but usually is a sentence containing the justification of the answer or a partial repetition of the proposition. It is often introduced by a verbal expression meaning "It does not surpass," "It is not difficult."

mubíkíriro. Prayers, which again are a form of poetry, are recited slowly and distinctly, the reciter pausing after each verse to permit the other celebrants to answer *aé* (yes) or to mumble *um*. Prayers are composed of many repetitious statements, which identify the names and epithets of the divinity or divinities invoked, give praise to the spirits, contain implorations for help, strength, good luck, good health, and success in hunting, and they make promises. They are recited by men—generally elders, headmen or other officeholders—without musical accompaniment, on various occasions, for example, before and after the hunt, at the blessing of departing relatives and of hunting dogs, during the dedication of persons or animals to divinities, on state occasions, and throughout the course of offerings and libations.

musínjo. Eulogistic recitations for chiefs, headmen, and mountains are given on state occasions by elders who are prominent in the political structure as headmen and officeholders and who are leading adepts of certain cults. The recitation, without musical accompaniment, is made in a staccato manner (words are split by the reciter into syllables or groups of two or three syllables) after which there is a short pause to permit participants to murmur *aé* or *um*. The content is monotonous and consists mainly of names, but the ethnohistorical knowledge and data about land and territorial divisions to be gained from them are very rewarding. The most impressive aspects of the eulogistic recitations, however, are to be found in the rhythm, the gestures, and the intense solidarity or *esprit de corps* manifested by the members of different groups.

ihamuriro. Stereotyped formulas, used in divination and medicinal practices, with highly esoteric overtones, are enunciated extremely quickly by specialists (diviners and medicine men) while interpreting oracles or preparing and applying medicine.

rwimbo. These are songs; all Nyanga songs are a form of poetry. As formerly mentioned and as revealed by those that occur in the Mwindo epic, the songs are basically concatenations of proverbs, improvised, terse statements made by the singer about his personal experiences, remembrances, as well as abstracts of tales. According to the social or ceremonial circumstances, highly different interpretations may be given for identical songs and only twin songs are among the more specialized ones. Both short and long songs are interspersed in the tales.

uano and *mushĭngá*. The first is a tale in general, the second a tale where the supernatural element, produced by the intervention of divinities, celestial bodies, monsters, and forest specters, stands in the foreground. Countless minor and major variants of the same tales are known, and everybody from adolescence on is able adequately to narrate or at least to summarize some of these tales. The dramatis personae in the tales are animals—all kinds of animals, but particularly the Duiker antelope, the turtle, the hunting dog, and the leopard. It is striking, however, that the most sacred animals, like the pangolin, the hornbill, the flying squirrel, the dendrohyrax, the bongo antelope, and the potto, are *never* included in these stories. In the tales there are human beings (particularly individuals who stand in a kinship or friendship relationship to one another, or chiefs and Pygmies). There are personified abstract characters (e.g., Shébuhányá, the Calamitous; Shéburongú, the Generous; Shébushú, the Man-of-Hatred). There are also extraordinary awe-inspiring beings like Kirĭmu, the Dragon; Mpacá the Forest Specter; Mukĭtĭ, the Water Serpent. Much more rarely are divinities or ancestors mentioned in these texts. Semideified celestial bodies and the elements (e.g., Moon, Star, Rain, Hail, Cloud) occasionally appear as principal or secondary actors in the tales. Tales are narrated, partly sung, mimed, and partly dramatized on a great variety of domestic, legal, ritual occasions to entertain, to instruct, to explain, to moralize. It would be inexact to isolate for any given tale a single one of these functions. Most, if not all, Nyanga tales simultaneously perform recreational, pedagogical, etiological, and moralizing roles, but specific situations may demand special emphasis on a single function.

nganuriro. These are "true stories" about partly imaginary, partly real events. Men, particularly trappers and hunters, are the experts in telling this type of story. In a terse style and a somewhat laconic tone, always speaking in the first person (singular or plural), men tell about things that happened to them or to their close relatives (the stories invariably begin with either "I (we) have seen . . ." or "I (we) have heard . . ." or "We were astonished . . ."). The occurrence of unusual events, the apparition of strange beings, the development of abnormal situations, or the ascription of extraordinary powers and skills to *known* persons are all depicted as real happenings. In this kind of "true stories" which are told in the men's meeting place, the embryos of new tales are found in the reports on long hunting or trapping expeditions or on a prolonged journey to a distant kinsman.

There are many other texts, which are generally not classified as literature, but which, as far as the Nyanga are concerned, fall into well-established categories according to content and style. They are the following:

mwanikiro. These are meditations, reflections expressed in a concise style. Many traces of these well-stated personal thoughts which are given in men's discussions are found in the songs. As already stated, Nyanga songs are essentially concatenations of proverbs and of such concisely formulated personal reflections.

kishámbáro. Discourses on or systematic coherent treatments of the problems of the country or state uttered by the elders, headmen, and chiefs.

ịhano. Instructions; teachings made to the youth about customs, skills, techniques, patterns of behavior. The texts are short, conceived in an easy, informal conversational style, and are generally introduced by the formula "we are accustomed to do. . . ." The stereotyped description and analysis of good and bad omens (*mwangiriro; kihunda*) and of taboos, prohibitions, and injunctions (*mutándo*) would also fall under this category of teachings and counsels.

kárịsị. These epic texts are few in number and are known to only a small number of men. The central hero in the Nyanga epics, as in the text presented here, is Mwindo. Mwindo is currently given as a personal name, in the family unit, to a male who is born after a number of girls. The Nyanga also see a relationship between the name and the verb *uindo*, to fell trees, thus emphasizing physical strength. Mwindo has several epithets, such as *Kábútwa-kénda* (the Little-one-just-born-he-walked) and *Mboru* (etymology unknown to the Nyanga). He is considered to be a small being, as is indicated by the diminutive prefix *ka-* by which he is designated throughout the epic. He is human, although he is not conceived and born as a normal human being (in some versions, he is a product of parthenogenesis; in other versions, he is born from sexual intercourse, but through his mother's medius). He is the son of a chief, rejected in some versions by his father, but ultimately he becomes chief; accepted by his father in other versions, he becomes chief after a partition of the state. He has fabulous gifts (he can move on land, in water, underground; he has the gift of premonition); he has powerful human, animal, and supernatural allies (paternal aunt, spiders, bats, lightning); he possesses by birth powerful magic objects (e.g., a *conga* flyswatter made from antelope or buffalo tail) which permit him to escape the worst difficulties. He is the destroyer of evil forces, the savior of people, a generous leader.

Kárịsị is the generic term for the long epic narratives that celebrate Mwindo's feats, but, interestingly, in one version of the epic, Kárịsị is also the name of a chief, who is married to the divinity of good fortune (Kahómbó) and whose son, born of parthenogenesis, is Mwindo, For a small group of individuals, those who participate in the performance, transmission, and preservation of the epic form of literary tradition, Kárịsị is a male spirit. When asked why he learned the epic, a Nyanga bard replies that he did so as the result of a compulsory message received in dreams from Kárịsị. This can be easily understood in the following terms. The patterns of transmission of epics are, of course, determined by kinship and friendship. Young men who are agnatic relatives, affines, and/or blood friends of the accomplished bard learn the epic in an informal way by accompanying him as helpers whenever he goes to recite. They are usually about three in number, but not all these young men will ultimately be expert in narrating the epic. It is likely that only one of them—the more energetic, intelligent, assiduous, better-liked one—will be fully instructed by the bard in the performance of the epic in all its complexity. If one of the bard's companions falls sick or suffers other frustrations (ill-fated hunting parties, death of near relatives, personal injuries), the oracles will surely ascribe his misfortune to Kárịsị's anger and dissatisfaction about the slowness and negligence with which he has been learning the epic. The cause of this evil fate can be removed only by appropriate devotions to Kárịsị. These devotions are accomplished in two ways: first, the accelerated learning of the epic text and its subsequent performance; second, the erection, behind the house, of a small table-like shrine (*busunị*) on which offerings and libations of banana beer are made. The bard and his colleagues and friends ceremonially drink banana beer, through an otherwise rarely used reed tube, from a gourd placed on the shrine.

The main emblems of the cult are an iron bell and a *butenge*-spear with copper rings fixed around the shaft. These objects are said to be carried by the spirit Kárịsị when, dressed in royal paraphernalia, he reveals himself in dreams. During offerings, the spear is planted near the shrine and the bell is attached to the gourd. During narration, the spear stands near the bard, while the bell may be fixed to his ankle. The bards themselves are called Kárịsị, which indicates, as is clear from other similar cultural practices, that they are devotees of the spirit Kárịsị or Shé-kárịsị, a name constructed like any tek-nonym, signifying that he is the "father of . . .," "possessor of . . .," "in control of . . .," or "maker of . . ." an epic story.

As shown by the translated text, the epic is said to be *cárwïmbo*, the song par excellence. Episode by episode, the epic is first sung, then narrated. While singing and narrating, the bard dances, mimes, and dramatically represents the main peripeties of the story. In this dramatic representation, the bard takes the role of the hero. The normal musical accompaniment consists of a percussion stick (*nkwángátiro*) which, resting on a few little sticks so as to have better resonance, is beaten with drumsticks by three young men (*bashénkwángátiro*). These men regularly accompany the bard when he performs; they are recruited among the members of the bard's own descent groups and/or his close affines (e.g., sororal nephew) or blood friends. They know large fragments of the epic, and, whenever necessary, help the bard to remember and to find the thread of his story. Eventually, one of them will acquire full knowledge and mastery of the text and be the bard's successor. The narrator himself shakes the calabash rattle (containing little seeds or pebbles) and carries anklet bells (*ntsụmbo*). The percussionists and members of the audience sing the refrains of the songs or repeat a whole sentence during each short pause made by the bard. In this capacity, they are called *barịsịya* (those who agree with . . .; those who say yes). Members of the audience also encourage the reciter with short exclamations (including onomatopoeia) and handclapping or whooping.

The Nyanga epic is not a text performed only at certain times or on highly esoteric ceremonial occasions. There is nothing secret about it; it is to be heard and enjoyed by all the people. Normally a chief or headman or simply the senior of a local descent group, in order to entertain his people and guests, would invite the bard to perform a few episodes of the epic in the evening, around the men's hut in the middle of the village. Large crowds of people, male and female, young and old, would come to listen or rather to be participant auditors. The bard and his collaborators would receive food and beer. During the performance, they would receive, not only from the host, but also from many auditors, *masabo*-gifts consisting mainly of small amounts of *butéá*-money, beads, and armlets. They would also receive, like any good musician or dancer or singer, the praises of the crowd, praises expressed in words and in gestures (symbolic drying of sweat, adjusting of the clothing, pulling of the fingers, and straightening of the back of the dancing narrator). There would not be any special fees paid to them at the end of the performance, although the bard might receive, like any other respected guest, a special farewell gift (*įkósórwa*). If excitement ran high and beer and food were plentiful, the narrator would be invited to continue parts of the narration on the following evening. The interesting point is that the narrator would never recite the entire story in immediate sequence, but would intermittently perform various select passages of it. Mr. Rureke, whose epic is presented here, repeatedly asserted that never before had he performed the whole story within a continuous span of days.

The epic incorporates most literary forms known to the Nyanga, in both poetry and prose: rigidly stereotyped enunciations and improvised remarks, songs consisting of proverbs, improvised reflections, riddles and abstracts of tales, songs that have the characteristics of praises, prayers, and blessings. The protagonist is a human hero (*muraį*), but he is surrounded by almost all categories of dramatis personae found in the tales: human beings (chiefs and officeholders, Pygmies, kinsmen, friends, and followers); animals (insects, fishes, birds, mammals), some of them his allies (spiders, bats, hawk) and some his enemies (fishes, crabs, aardvark); fabulous beings (the Water Serpent Mukįtį and the Dragon Kirįmu); divinities (Kahómbó, Muisa, Nkúbá); personified, and sometimes semi-deified, celestial bodies and the elements (Moon, Star, Rain, Hail, Cloud). The content of the epic is a rich survey of customs, institutions, activities, behavior patterns, values, material objects that are of main significance to the Nyanga. It is, in fact, a synopsis of Nyanga culture. Functionally the epic is many things: entertainment, moralization, an explanation of causes, and an interpretation of existing customs; it is a paideia.

Finally, what is presented here as a piece of oral literature is much more than that. It is music, rhythm, song, dance, movement, dramatic entertainment. It is feasting and gift-giving (those who present the gifts dance and gesticulate). It is group solidarity and mass participation. For the bard himself, the act of narrating the story has religious significance. He believes that Kárjsj, deified, wanted him to learn the epic; to perform the drama adequately makes the narrator "strong," protects him against disease and death. The narrator believes he will find in his songs the force that Mwindo himself, the hero of the epic, derives from them.

THE NARRATOR, MR. SHÉ-KÁRJSJ
CANDI RUREKE

I met Mr. Rureke, narrator of the Mwindo epic, in Bese. Extremely isolated, far away from roads, located in a dense forest area that is infested with big game and intersected by numerous rivers, Bese is famous for its hunters, trappers, and fishermen, and for its great tradition of blacksmithing. Composed of sixty-four huts and nine outlying hamlets, the village is fairly large in size. Male representatives of not less than sixteen different descent groups live in the village which is traditionally placed under the headmanship of a member of the Bacira descent group. Bese is part of a small traditional state called Rare or cǔo cáBana-Kabákj, which, as is common among the Nyanga, consists of only a couple of villages and their outlying hamlets. The state is ruled by one of the few surviving sacred chiefs, Mwanankuyu. As a result of repeated and systematic regrouping and resettling of people by the Belgian administration, this and other petty states in the northwestern part of Nyanga country were merged into a single administrative unit, known as *groupement Kisimba*. A region of exceptionally dense rain forest called Ihímbí cuts across the boundaries of the Rare and other states. This region, which ecologically is but a southeastward extension of the huge rain forest that covers the adjoining territories of Lubutu, Bafwasende, Mambasa, and part of Lubero, was originally occupied by Pygmies, few of whom remained in the area because of emigration or absorption into Nyanga ranks. According to Nyanga traditions, the first peoples to encounter the Pygmies in these areas were collectively known as Bahímbí. These Bahímbí are part of a cluster of peoples living in areas adjoining Nyanga country and are known in ethnographical records as Bapiri, Bamate, Batįrį. Nyanga groups, immigrating from the east (Rutshuru territory), later settled in this area and established political control over it. As a result of this contact, the Bahímbí, who were already strongly influenced by the Pygmies, were culturally assimilated by the Nyanga. Nyanga culture predominates among the few groups still known as Bahímbí, but they differ from most other Nyanga in that they are heavily specialized in big-game hunting. Mr. Rureke, by his kinship origins, belongs to such a group.

As shown in the first lines of this epic, the region of Ihímbí forms the setting within which the action takes place. In his last song, the narrator even praises Ihímbí: *MwiHímbí kwįtų́ nongóbo/in Ihimbi, in our country it is fine.* The fact, then, is that Rureke possessed a house in the village of Bese and that he resided there, but Bese was not his home village. A member of the Bana-nkurį descent group, Rureke was born in the village of Koutu which was located in the heart of Ihímbí before it was abandoned in about 1931, both as the result of boundary disputes and of administrative resettlement of scattered groups. Before the colonial era, Koutu had been the center of a petty state called cǔo cáBana-Koumbo. The male members of Rureke's descent group were classified as the perpetual maternal uncles of the local ruling line of Baruko chiefs. The abandonment of Koutu resulted in the dispersal of its descent groups. Rureke, his two uterine junior brothers, Butinda and Muhiirwa, and two members of the Baruko group settled in Bese.

It would be incorrect to think of Rureke as a "stranger" in Bese village, for he was linked by various ties to many of its inhabitants. First, there had always been close political ties rooted in kinship between the rulers of Kouto and Rare. Second, Rureke's maternal uncles (the Baherį) and his in-laws (the Bafúý̨ or Babúý̨) were established in Bese. Third, Rureke had personal relationships, founded in distant kinship and in friendship, with two men of considerable influence in the village. Both men, Risaki Kangakora (the senior son of the village headman) and Butinda (a son of the headman's senior brother) of the Bacira group, were classificatory sororal nephews of the Baruko. Rureke, as a member of a group that stood in a perpetual relationship of maternal uncles to the Baruko, was automatically considered to be a classificatory grandfather of both men. This relationship was enhanced by some special form of *esprit de corps* arising from the fact that all three men had been working for European concerns, located not too far from Nyanga country.

Rureke, a youthful-looking man about fifty years old, was not wealthy, nor did he hold any political or ritual office. In contrast with his junior brothers, he had only one wife; she was sick and resided with her two children in the hamlet of Bese, which was occupied by members of her own descent group, the Bafúÿá or Babúÿá. Rureke depended for his food on the wives of his junior brothers and of his two friends. In his youth, Rureke had been a skillful maker of mats and baskets and that is how he got his name (which literally means basket). Then he had become a helper of Kanyangara of Bese, who was an expert narrator of the Mwindo epic. Kanyangara, who belonged to the Bafúÿá or Babúÿá descent group, had blood brotherhood relationships with Rureke's father; Rureke's father also selected a wife for his son from this group. On several occasions, Rureke refers in the songs to the fact that he has learned his story from the Babúÿá (his pronunciation of Bafúÿá), thus paying tribute to his teacher:

> *Twanánge múano*
> We are telling (from) the story
> *Rwánángá Babúÿá*
> That the Babuya have told (long ago).

and

> *Tuané kwaruano*
> Let us recite from the story
> *Runaáná Babúÿá*
> That the Babuya are used to reciting.

Rureke knew only that Kanyangara had learned the epic from a certain Bishusha whom he could not further identify.

From Rureke's social background it is clear that the epic he knew had its roots in a region where three cultural traditions (Pygmies, Bahímbí, Nyanga) had been intimately integrated with one another. The Nyanga insist that the Pygmies were at one time great bards who performed *kárịsị*-like stories for their chiefs. They do not, however, say that these stories originated with the Pygmies. On the other hand, it is interesting to note that Rureke, the only great performer of the Mwindo epic alive in Nyanga country in the mid-fifties, had, through his kinship origins, very deep roots in an area that all Nyanga agree was once occupied by Pygmies. It is also significant that Rureke learned the epic from a member of the Bafúÿá (Babúÿá) whose original name they themselves assert was Bana-Mutwá (an appellation that contains the word for Pygmy).

Throughout the epic Mwindo is designated and designates himself as a small creature (systematic use of the *ka-* diminutive prefix). Given the fantastic attributes of the miraculously born hero, there is no reason that he could not have grown rapidly or have been born to full size. This fact may also indicate Pygmy influence.[3] The Pygmies figure in Rureke's epic as the hero's loyal hunters; in other, but shorter or fragmentary, versions of the Mwindo epic, the role of the Pygmies is elaborated upon much more. In one of them, Mwindo is represented as a great hunter, going on fabulous expeditions with his fourteen Pygmies and two dogs.

According to P. Schebesta, the Kibira-speaking Basúa Pygmies and also the southern Efe Pygmies have a divinity known by the name of Kalisia.[4] It is tempting to see a connection between this name and the Nyanga Kárįsį (which is, as we have stated, the generic term for epic, the name of a chief said to be the father of Mwindo in one version of the epic and the name of a divinity worshiped only by the bards). The Pygmy Kalisia is characterized as the lord of the forest and of game, as the protector of hunters who guides their search for animals and helps in killing them. He also appears in dreams, giving counsel about trails of animals and places to set up hunting camps. During the ceremonies of the cult, a spear is planted near the offering pole.[5] The elements of dream and spear are also present in the Nyanga worship of Kárįsį. Moreover, the hero Mwindo himself possesses the basic characteristic that the Pygmies ascribe to Kalisia: in Nyanga, Mwindo is a *minéntsí*, a master of the path, a leader who knows in advance of things to come.

---

3. According to Schebesta, the Pygmy Tore, divinity, ancestor, culture hero, is also small (P. Schebesta, *Les Pygmées du Congo Belge* [Brussels: Académie royale des Sciences d'Outre-Mer, 1952], p. 305; see also H. Tegnaeus, *Le héros civilisateur* [Uppsala, 1950], p. 165).

4. Schebesta, *op. cit.*, pp. 303–306.

5. *Ibid.*, pp. 303–306.

The customs, institutions, values, behavior patterns described and suggested in the Mwindo epic are consistently Nyanga; however, epithets and recurrent detailed descriptions of physical traits and emotions are infrequent in the rest of Nyanga literature. The contention is not that the Mwindo epic originated with the Pygmies, but that the Nyanga incorporated several themes, dramatis personae, and functions that they adopted and adapted from the Pygmies and also possibly from the Bapiri-Batjrj-Bamate cluster.

THE MWINDO EPIC

The text presented here is by far the longest, most comprehensive, most coherent, most detailed, and most poetic of all versions of the Mwindo story which I heard in Nyanga country.[6] The themes of the epic are typical, but neither exclusive nor exhaustive of the feats generally ascribed to the hero Mwindo. In other words, there are, according to the different versions of the epic, variations in the hero's alliances and struggles and in the details of his life story. The miraculous birth into the chief's family, the conflict with the father (though usually less circumstantially analyzed), the aid of the maternal uncles and the maternal aunt, the alliance with animals, the friendship with the Pygmies, the Herculean tasks imposed by the divinities, the *wiki*-game, the ascent and/or descent of the hero to the supernatural realm—all are common themes. In some versions, however, the Pygmies play a much more active and significant role throughout the epic, more of the story moves in the supernatural realm, there is a larger number of imaginary beings (normally absent from Nyanga tales and religion) such as Ukanga (Big Rock), Kabaraka (alleged brother of Lightning), Musero (White Rock), Itembe (Wild Banana Tree). Elsewhere, Mwindo has a sister Nyamitondo who is married to Lightning and who sometimes assumes the role played by the paternal aunt here. In still another version where the temporary metamorphosis of human beings and divinities into hunted animals is a constant theme, Mwindo is a great hunter and is exposed by the god of fire to a number of tests.

6. I have recorded five other versions of the epic: one is a complete story but is half as long as this text; the second is still shorter and confused (the old narrator did not adequately remember the text); the three others are fragmentary.

In this version, too, Mwindo gets help, not from his living paternal aunt, but from her spirit.

In our version of the epic, Mwindo identifies himself in dialogues and songs as *Kábútwa-kénda* (the Little-one-just-born-he-walked), but there is one version in which Mwindo and *Kábútwa-kénda* are two different persons, related to each other as half brothers, Mwindo being the false hero. In that version, *Kábútwa-kénda* is born by parthenogenesis, whereas Mwindo is born of the chief's ritual wife in normal fashion. *Kábútwa-kénda*, described as a great singer and musician liked by women, wins all battles against Mwindo, yet is generous, providing his brother with a wife and a village and bringing him back to life after he died. After *Kábútwa-kénda*'s death, the astute Mwindo usurps the throne destined for his paternal nephew Buingo wa-Ngoma. In his unwillingness to return power to his nephew, as stipulated by the oracles, Mwindo causes the death of his own child. The dead child, however, obtains the death of its father (Mwindo) after his arrival in the Underworld.

In our epic, a synthesis is made of all the feats and attributes of Mwindo and *Kábútwa-kénda* and all are ascribed to Mwindo: he is astute, strong, miraculously born; he is wronged by his father; he has the help of certain animals, of his maternal uncles, and of his aunt; he is a great singer whose songs have a magic force; he is successful in battle; yet, he is not a perfect hero, since without his magic scepter, the help of Lightning, the help of his aunt and uncles, the help of certain animals (hawk, sparrow, spiders, bats, hedgehog), the help of his *kahombo* (good fortune), he would not be able to confront all his opponents; ultimately he changes in character from a boaster to a wise, generous, benevolent ruler.

The Nyanga have no titles for their tales or subtitles under which to indicate the various episodes of the epic narrative. We have, therefore, presented the text as one continuous entity. In order to give a better idea of the various actors and their functions, of the various themes and situations described, I present a synoptic table of contents.

I. The Setting

A. Temporal and spatial

The events take place in remote times in a known place, the state of Ihímbí, the village of Tubondo (which, as its name indicates, is a place of many raphia trees and, as is implied elsewhere in the epic, is located on a hill or mountain). The main action takes place in the village of

Tubondo; it is there that the epic begins and there that it ends; it is the place to which the action returns at the four turning points of the epic. The sequence of locations in which the events take place is:

> Village of Tubondo
> Pool or dwelling place of the Water Serpent Mukiti
> Village of Tubondo
> River dominated by Mukiti's allies
> Village of Tubondo
> Subterranean world of Muisa, Ntumba, Sheburungu
> Village of Tubondo
> Deep forest
> Village of Tubondo
> Celestial realm of Lightning, Rain, Hail, Moon, Sun, Star
> Village of Tubondo

The spatial plan of the epic corresponds closely to the Nyanga conception of the division of the universe into four spheres: *butú* (sky), *mwanyá* (atmosphere), *oto* (earth), *kwirúngá* (underworld). The actors move and the actions take place in these four spheres: Star puts the hero in the sphere of *butú;* the contacts with Lightning bring him to the less distant sphere of *mwanyá;* the subterranean journey to Muisa, Ntumba, Sheburungu is in the *kwirúngá* sphere; the rest of the action takes place on earth, the *oto* sphere. Earth itself has four subdivisions: *kumbúka* (the village; the inhabited world), *kubusará* (the deep forest), *kumundụra* (the forest, clearings, fields near the village), *kundǔsi* (the water). Action occurs in all these places, but it is centered in the village.

B. The key dramatis personae

Chief Shemwindo and his seven wives (among whom are a preferred wife and a despised one); the chief's sister, Iyangura, paternal aunt of the unborn hero; the hero, whose name is not mentioned in the beginning, but who is already known as Mwindo because of the teknonymic name by which the chief is called.

As the action moves on, a great many other actors are drawn in besides the inner circle of kinsmen. They fall into six categories.

1. *Humans*
   Unnamed group of nobles, counselors, and commoners, of midwives, of old and young people

Maidservants of Iyangura
Drummers and singers of Mwindo
Pygmies of Mwindo

2. *Animals*
   On the hero's side: the Spiders, the Bats, the Hedgehog, the Sparrow
   Opposed to the hero: the fishes, prominent among them Kasiyembe (the guardian of the hero's aunt); the cricket
   Ambiguous: the Hawk
   Semideified, enemy of the hero: Ntumba or Aardvark

3. *Divinities*
   Inimical to the hero: Muisa and Sheburungu
   Friend and ally of the hero (but in the earliest stage of the epic working against him): Nkuba
   Ambiguous: Kahindo, daughter of Muisa; Musoka, sister of Mukiti
   Friendly, but not allied: Kentse, Sun; Mweri, Moon

4. *Semideified elements*
   Friendly, but not allied: Rain, Hail, Cloud, Star

5. *Fabulous beings*
   Hostile, but never in direct conflict with hero: Mukiti, the Water Serpent
   Enemy of the hero's Pygmies, destroyed by hero: Kirimu, the dragon

6. *Mystical objects that help the hero in his struggles*
   Conga: scepter made from buffalo or antelope tail, to which hero owes in final instance all his power
   Bag of good fortune
   Rope
   Axe

C. The intentional and simultaneous pregnancies of the chief's seven wives

D. The unmotivated interdiction and threat by the chief that the seven wives should not bear males

*II. Interlude: The Marriage of Iyangura, the Hero's Paternal
Aunt, to Mukiti, the Mythical Water Serpent*

The action takes place both in the village of Tubondo (courtship, marriage negotiations, gift exchanges, transfer of valuables) and in the village of the Water Serpent (exposé of marriage plans, accumulation of matrimonial goods, actual marriage ceremony). This very beautiful and poetic interlude, which is absent from other versions of the epic, gives a fairly accurate description of marriage customs, and strongly emphasizes the basic Nyanga values of generosity, hospitality, and refinement in social relationships. The passage is full of unusually rich imagery, rarely, if ever, found in the rest of Nyanga literature, suggesting the beauty of both Iyangura and Mukiti and the intensity of their mutual passion. The interlude contains at least three elements of main significance for the development of the epic. First, it gives a justification for the absence from the village of the hero's aunt, a person who in Nyanga practice could have exercised strong pressures against her ill-inspired brother. Second, it gives special status and power to Iyangura, because she is depicted as Mukiti's ritual wife (*mumbo*); from many points of view, the ritual wife has the powers and privileges of the chief. Third, because as a ritual wife she lives in separation from her husband (a normal Nyanga practice), the freedom of decision and action which she shows throughout the story is fully justified.

III. The Hero's Miraculous Birth; his Attributes and First Exploits

The action takes place in and around the village of the hero's birth, Tubondo.

A. As prescribed by the chief, six of his (the chief's) seven wives bear daughters.

B. The preferred wife does not give birth; she is mocked by the people and is anxious about her fate.

C. The unborn hero performs several domestic tasks for his mother (brings firewood, water, vegetables).

D. In meditation, the unborn hero decides upon the time and manner of his birth; he appears through his mother's medius, but his mother has the pains of child delivery.

E. Complot of the midwives: they refuse to reveal the child's sex to the chief and his counselors.

F. Naming of the child: Mwindo (boy following a series of girls).

G. Betrayal of child's sex by cricket.

H. Apparition of the hero's father as a villain and the hero's reactions.

> Father throws spear into the hut, but hero's word has magic force: "May this spear end up at the bottom of the housepole. . . ."
>
> Father has his counselors bury the hero, but the latter, in the grave, warns his father of his own coming sufferings; at night a strong light is visible from the grave, and the hero escapes to go back to his mother's hut.
>
> In the middle of this passage, the narrator has inserted the enumeration of the mystic objects and supernatural gifts with which the hero was born (*conga*-scepter, adze, bag of good fortune, rope, capacity to speak and laugh from birth on).
>
> Father has his counselors make a drum, imprison the hero in it, and throw him in a pool (the realm of Mukiti); there is rain and hail for seven days, also famine.
>
> The hero's mother is despised by her husband.

I. Meditations of the hero in the drum.

J. In a song, the hero reveals to the young maidens of Tubondo his coming journey and his goal to find his paternal aunt.

K. In another song, the hero repeats for his father and his father's counselors his plan of action.

IV. The Hero's Aquatic Journey in Search of his Paternal Aunt

The action takes place in a river that is the realm of the mythical Water Serpent Mukiti. The hero travels in the drum beneath the surface of the water and, at one moment, in the sand underneath the riverbed.

A. By means of a magic song, the boasting hero subdues the various species of fishes and crabs which, as Mukiti's allies, block the road. For the first time, in this song, the hero gives himself the epithet of *Kábútwa-kénda* (the Little-one-just-born-he-walked).

B. Encounter with the snake divinity Musoka, identified here as the junior sister of Mukiti. Mwindo speaks in a soft voice to this woman, who, uncertain about her role, asks her brother for advice. Finally, Mwindo is compelled to avoid her barrage by traveling past it underneath the riverbed.

C. The hero's encounter with Mukiti "at the knot where Mukiti was coiled up." Mwindo identifies himself as Iyangura's child; maidens at the wading place bring the news to Iyangura.

D. Encounter with Iyangura: informed by the maidservants, Iyangura, following a path bordering the river, goes to see for herself. Mwindo reveals himself and his goals in a song, but Iyangura, to be more sure about his identity, exposes him to tricky questioning. When she identifies him "as the sororal nephew of the Bats," the drum leaves the water and Iyangura slashes the membrane and Mwindo is freed. He appears as "multiple rays of the rising sun and of the moon."

E. Betrayal by Hawk: Kasiyembe, the guardian of Iyangura, is informed by Hawk about the encounter of Mwindo and Iyangura.

F. Encounter of the hero with the villain Kasiyembe, "the man of hatred."

Kasiyembe challenges Mwindo; Hedgehog informs Mwindo about the traps set for him by Kasiyembe and builds a tunnel that will permit the hero to avoid the traps and go directly to his aunt's house.

Mwindo takes up Kasiyembe's threat and sends his aunt home, inviting her to warn Kasiyembe.

Spider builds bridges across the traps,

Mwindo arrives in his aunt's house through the tunnel.

Iyangura's duplicity: although she knows about her husband's deceitful plans, she does not permit Mwindo to eat, but urges him to dance, as requested by Kasiyembe.

Mwindo's successful dance above the pits and his provocative song; during this dance, for the first time, the hero agitates his *conga*-scepter, which with the help given by the Spider's bridges gives him a double immunity.

Kasiyembe implores Nkuba for help, but Mwindo's words again have force and Nkuba strikes in vain.

By sheer volition, Mwindo sets fire to Kasiyembe's hair; those who try to extinguish the flames can find no water, not even saliva.

At Iyangura's imploration, Mwindo wakes Kasiyembe by means of a song and his *conga*-scepter.

Kasiyembe praises and blesses Mwindo.

V. *The Hero's Return to his Natal Village Tubondo; his Father's Flight; the Destruction of Tubondo*

The action consecutively takes place in Iyangura's hamlet, on the trail leading to Tubondo, in the village of the hero's maternal uncles, in a glen facing Tubondo, and in Tubondo itself. Mwindo is no longer a lonely traveler; he is accompanied by his paternal aunt and her maid-servants who are joined in the course of the trip by Mwindo's maternal uncles, the Bats.

A. Mwindo announces his plan to return to his home village to fight with his father.

B. His aunt is skeptical about the issue, yet decides to accompany him together with her servants.

C. Songs are sung along the way in which the boasting hero warns his father about his coming.

D. The hero stays overnight in the village of his maternal uncles; his body is forged by them at his own request. Skeptical about Mwindo's fight, they decide to accompany him.

E. Mwindo and his followers are compelled to spend the night in the glen below the mountain on which Tubondo is built. It is cold and rainy; the people are hungry. Again sheer volition and a long, compelling song permit Mwindo to provide his followers with shelter, food, and implements. In this passage there is a succinct inventory of Nyanga material culture provided by a long song in which Mwindo compels all objects and animals in his father's village to join him in the glen.

F. Mwindo sends his uncles to fight in Tubondo; all but one, who brings the news about the catastrophe, are wiped out.

G. Mwindo alone sets out to Tubondo "to find out the reason why my uncles are all wiped out," leaving his bag, his axe, and his rope to his aunt.

H. Arriving in Tubondo, he wants to dance, but is not allowed to do so and is insulted. In a long song, he again explains his grievances, then asks for Lightning's intervention.

I. Lightning destroys Tubondo, wiping out all its inhabitants, but Shemwindo manages to escape underground through the root of a *kikoka*-fern.

J. Mwindo gets his aunt and her servants, establishing them in Tubondo; he brings his maternal uncles back to life and wills all animals, implements, foods back from the glen.

VI. Mwindo's Subterranean Journey in Search of his Father

The action takes place underground, where the Nyanga locate the larger number of their divinities. Alone, because all others "are used to eating terrestrial foods," Mwindo enters the Underworld through the root of a *kikoka*-fern and travels into the realms of Muisa ("place where no one ever clusters around the fire"), of Ntumba, Aardvark, and of Sheburungu (one of the epithets under which the supreme divinity of fire, Nyamurairi, is known).

A. Mwindo, by some form of clairvoyance, knows that his father has fled to the realm of Muisa.

B. He takes leave of his aunt, but maintains contact with her by means of the rope with which he was born.

C. Sparrow points out the kikoka-fern at whose root Shemwindo entered the Underworld.

D. Encounter at a wading place with Kahindo, daughter of Muisa, covered with yaws.

> Mwindo explains his intentions.
>
> He gets magic formulas from her which will permit him to escape Muisa's tricky invitations to sit down, to drink banana beer, and to eat banana paste.
>
> He heals the yaws of Kahindo.

E. Encounter with Muisa.

> Mwindo successfully escapes the tricky language of Muisa.
>
> He rests and eats in Kahindo's house.
>
> Muisa imposes upon him the Herculean task of clearing the forest, cultivating and harvesting bananas in a single day.
>
> Mwindo successfully carries out the various tasks, but, about to return with the bananas to Muisa's village, he is subdued by Muisa's magic belt, then saved by his own *conga*-scepter.
>
> Mwindo comforts his aunt, who, feeling the rope become still, thinks he is dead.
>
> He sends his *conga*-scepter to smash Muisa, then arrives with the bananas in the village and awakens Muisa at his daughter's request.

Muisa, revivified, sends him out on honey-harvesting and again, seeing his success, has him smashed against a tree by his magic belt, but Mwindo is brought back to life by his *conga*-scepter and brought down from the tree by Lightning. Muisa now sends a boy for Shemwindo, even though he has permitted Shemwindo to flee.

Hawk informs Mwindo about Muisa's betrayal and Shemwindo's flight.

Mwindo has Muisa smashed by his *conga*-scepter and leaves in search of his father.

F. Encounter with Aardvark (Ntumba).

Mwindo explains his plans in a song; he asks for the help of lightning.

While Mwindo is unable to enter Ntumba's cave, Ntumba has Shemwindo flee to Sheburungu.

Lightning destroys Ntumba's cave.

Hawk informs Mwindo about Shemwindo's flight.

Mwindo curses Ntumba ("May you never again find food in this country of yours"), but does not otherwise act against him.

G. Encounter with Sheburungu.

The hero meets hungry little children at the entrance of the village; he asks for and receives food from his distant aunt.

Mwindo plays the *wiki*-game with Sheburungu; he stakes and loses everything; when, however, he wagers his *conga*-scepter, luck turns in his favor.

At that very moment, Sparrow and Hawk inform the hero that his father is again trying to flee.

H. Encounter with father.

"They" (unspecified) lay hold of him.

Restraint and moderation on Mwindo's part: no insults, no violence.

VII. Mwindo's Subterranean Journey Home in the Company of his Father

Again, the villages of Sheburungu, Aardvark, and Muisa are the setting, until the hero emerges from the underground realms at the root of the *kikoka*-fern. It is unclear whether Mwindo carries his father during this trip or whether he is simply with him, for the verb *niríte* used in this context has a double meaning: lit., "I am carrying," but fig.,

"I have, I possess," as when one says in Nyanga that he has (carries) a wife or matrimonial goods.

- A. Mwindo returns to Sheburungu all goods won from him in gambling: Sheburungu blesses him.
- B. Mwindo informs his aunt about his coming return.
- C. Mwindo relates his own life story to Ntumba, who has rebuilt his cave; he is blessed by Ntumba.
- D. In a song, Mwindo reminds his aunt of his coming return.
- E. At Kahindo's request, Mwindo awakens Muisa; he reveals the mystery of his birth to Muisa.
- F. Mwindo reminds his aunt of his coming return.
- G. Mwindo rejects Muisa's proposal that Mwindo marry his daughter Kahindo.
- H. He emerges at the root of the *kikoka*-fern.

VIII. Mwindo as Ruler of Tubondo

The setting is the village of Tubondo, first in its state of destruction, inhabited only by Mwindo's aunt, maternal uncles, and helpers, and then as rebuilt and revivified by Mwindo with its seven descent groups. The circumstances are solemn: big statewide gathering of people and enthronement rites.

- A. Mwindo is greeted on arrival by his aunt and maternal uncles and seated by them on many spearheads.
- B. In a long song, Mwindo narrates his feats.
- C. Hospitality is given by Mwindo to his father: the father is accommodated in a guesthouse, and receives a goat and rice. Mwindo has abandoned his boasting; in a calm and dignified tone, he simply points out to his father that he made a big mistake.
- D. For three days, Mwindo, at Iyangura's request, brings all the people of Tubondo back to life, dancing to drums beaten by his maternal uncles and waving his *conga*-scepter. All the people of the village come to life pursuing the same activities as they were when they died.
- E. At Iyangura's insistence, Shemwindo calls together a big council.

F. Solemn opening of the council: apparition of the "three radiant Stars," Iyangura, Mwindo, Shemwindo; their installation on copper chairs suspended from the sky by Nkuba; invocation for strength and praise of the participants by Mwindo.

G. Speeches by Shemwindo, who publicly recognizes his errors; by Iyangura, who justifies her departure from Mukiti's's village and criticizes her brother; by Mwindo, who in a merciful mood asks for harmony and peace.

H. Decision to split the state into two parts to be ruled by Shemwindo and Mwindo.

I. Enthronement of Mwindo.

J. Departure of Iyangura; the blessing of Mwindo.

IX. The Dragon Hunt

The action takes place in the forest and in the village. The actors are the Dragon (Kirimu), the Pygmies, and Mwindo. Most versions known to me describe the fight with the Dragon. Numerous Nyanga tales deal with this theme: the Dragon is represented as a ruthless, man-eating, but somewhat stupid monster, which is sometimes killed by a little child.

A. Mwindo's Pygmies on a hunting party are swallowed by Kirimu, except one, Nkurongo, who brings Mwindo the news.

B. Mwindo overcomes the Dragon with a song of defiance and with his *conga*-scepter.

C. Mwindo's *conga* flies through the air to collect people to carry the monster back to the village.

D. The Dragon is carried to the village, cut up, distributed (with the injunction that every part be eaten); many people are liberated from the monster's belly.

E. Finally, the eyes are roasted and from each, as it bursts in a splatter, come a thousand people.

F. Lightning, who without Mwindo's knowledge had made a blood pact, smells the roasting eyes and decides to put his ally Mwindo to the test.

30   INTRODUCTION

X. Mwindo's Celestial Journey

The action takes place in space that is successively represented as a desolate place of severe cold and of extreme heat. The duration of the journey, rarely explicitly indicated, is one year.

A. Mwindo, singing and confident about the outcome, is lifted into the sky by Lightning. "Here there is no room for his heroism"; the hero is reduced to a passive, suffering subject, exposed to icy winds, great heat, and thirst. He is successively taken into the realms of Lightning, Rain, Hail, Moon, Sun, Star. Before being permitted to return to earth, the hero receives the order never again to kill an animal and to accept Lightning as his guardian.

B. Mwindo is returned to earth by Lightning.

C. He relates in a song and a speech his celestial experiences. Joy and life come back to the village which had been mourning ever since Mwindo's departure.

XI. Mwindo's Glory

A. Mwindo announces his message of prosperity and gives his commandments for an ordered life (no quarrels; no adultery; no mockery; awe for the chief; respect on the part of the chief for his subjects; solidarity; fertility).

B. Mwindo, a well-settled chief, rules in peace over his country and receives the allegiance of many strangers.

XII. The Narrator's Conclusions

A. "There is nothing bad in what God has given to man."

B. Excess leads to destruction.

C. Everybody needs advice.

D. Solidarity and mutual help save the people; there is no true authority without these.

E. There is no absolute power.

Few personality traits are explicitly mentioned in the text. The epithets themselves generally bear on physical characteristics or on political status of the actors: for example, the water serpent Mukiti is *mịné-márịba*, lord of the pools; Shemwindo is *nyeré-kurwábo*, master of their (country, village); Nkuba, the divinity of lightning, is *mirábyo*, flashes. The principal epithet of Mwindo himself, *Kábútwa-kénda*, stresses his capacity to walk from birth on. At least three physical traits are explicitly mentioned for Mwindo. He is small: *kabóntsóbóntso*, a small baby; *mwăna wémwịyoroyo*, just yesterday's child; *ubútwǎyo tété-tétéyo*, just born a while ago. He is beautiful; for example, when his aunt opened the drum in which Mwindo was imprisoned, she saw "the many rays of the rising sun and the moon. That is the beauty of the child Mwindo." He is a virile man; that is, he can act and talk like a full-fledged adult male. Different characters call him *wábŭme*, a man of poise (a concept that emphasizes his full manhood), or *wábŭme ukeráá byăra*, a man who has (his) nails cut (a concept that stands in opposition to the image of the ill-inspired, pernicious forest specter Mpacá, whose nails are never cut). For Hawk, Mwindo is *kárí ná mishịnga kakịrị*, with stories (feats) great; for Mukiti he is *wátáríké tu*, he surpasses all expectations; for Musoka, he is *mutáre*, a hero.

The context of the story implicitly indicates many other traits of Mwindo's personality. On the one hand, he is an excessive boaster, intrepid, arrogant, verbose, highly self-conscious, and ruthless, and, as such, he is largely unacceptable and somewhat unreal to the Nyanga, for truly great men (chiefs, headmen, great hunters) avoid boasting about their strength and skill. On the other hand, Mwindo is generous, magnanimous, and righteous. Although verbose, he rarely misuses words (e.g., to curse or to slander; he does so only when Muisa exaggerates in testing him: "stay like that, you dog"). Although threatening, he rarely is truly angry or irreconcilable (he first destroys his enemies, then permits them to live again; contemplating his destructive work, he remarks that "he would heal him when he would be back from where he was going"). Although ruthless in his search for his father, he bears him no grudge. Although often hard, his attitude toward his mother is tender (she is referred to as *nya-mwako*, mother of the cradling rope, an honorific term) and his attitude is pious toward his aunt and his father. The first Mwindo is evident as long as the search for his father lasts; the second one is best revealed after his father is found. But, even at the climax of his boisterous arrogance,

Mwindo occasionally shows tenderness (for his aunt) and generosity (for the hungry children and for a suffering female spirit). Even at the peak of his generosity (when he brings people back to life, returning all the goods won in games), Mwindo still gives proof of his excessive ruthlessness by killing three people who criticized him. The hero achieves his full fame and glory, *nkúrú*—his full acceptability in Nyanga eyes—only through catharsis in the celestial realm where he is a mere passive and suffering subject.

Mwindo's father is depicted as an ill-advised coward and weakling, the opposite of what a chief should be; Mwindo's aunt is talkative and insecure, but outspoken and fair in defending her nephew's cause and full of solicitude for him.

Several key Nyanga values are, directly or indirectly, stressed in the epic. The value of restraint and moderation is emphasized in the conclusions drawn by the narrator; there is a passage in which Mwindo's aunt explicitly asks Mwindo to practice restraint (*sicá émutíma*: bring down your heart); Mwindo achieves full glory only when he has gone through a catharsis that frees him from all excesses. This value runs like a leitmotiv through much of Nyanga thinking, indeed through much of the thinking of several other populations of the Kivu Province (e.g., the Lega, among whom it is the basic theme of all precepts given in the teachings of the *bwami*-association). Nyanga tales relate the episode of the aquatic bird *bishóbishó*, which had its nest built in the reeds near a lake and claimed to be the only important being in the world. The lake swallowed the bird's nest and eggs; the oracles taught the bird to say: "I am important but only in the company of the lake." Mwindo achieves full *karamo* (life force) and *nkúrú* (fame and force) only when he has definitely abandoned his boisterous, megalomaniacal behavior. So long as he is not purified of it, he is not an absolute hero; he is protected owing to the presence of his aunt or because of his *conga*-scepter or bag of good fortune or song (Mwindo is not strong, but the song itself is powerful, as when in other tales *weak* creatures escape severe dangers because of the force of their song). The values of hospitality and generosity are strongly emphasized (there is much reference to providing visitors with a house in which to sleep, with food and gifts); Mwindo is generous toward his aunt, his uncles, young children, and even his enemies. Kinship solidarity (reflected in the relationships between Mwindo and his aunt, Mwindo and his maternal uncles, and ultimately in the relationship between father and son) and friendship (e.g., Mwindo's reliance upon his friend Lightning) are constantly placed in the foreground. Poised and well-informed leadership is also of great importance (Shemwindo's hatred against his son causes nothing but destruction and misery for himself and for his people and allies; Mwindo's poise and wisdom ultimately produce happiness and glory). Against a background of many boisterous threats, there is insistence on the choice usage of words (e.g., in the highly select and precise usage of reciprocal kinship terms, honorific epithets, euphemisms, and extremely rare verbal curses).

The idea of good life is synthesized by the term *karamo*, often used in the text, which means good health, strength, force, salvation, good life (*karamo* is derived from *irama*, to recover, to heal). *Karamo* is the current greeting among the Nyanga; it is also a central theme in invocations, prayers, and other cultual practices. When, at the end of so many peripeties and successes, Iyangura returns to her husband's village, there is nothing left for her but to wish that her nephew may be in full possession of *karamo*. To have *karamo* means to be healthy, to be wise, to be free of passions, to have many children, to be successful in hunting, to entertain smooth social relationships.

The Mwindo epic is a coherent, well-balanced, well-constructed story told in a rich language, enhanced by the poetic talent of the narrator, Mr. Rureke. It incorporates all the literary styles known to the Nyanga. It contains a succinct survey of many basic institutions and customs, some described in detail, others merely suggested or implied (e.g., kinship terminology, patterns of behavior between kinsmen, marriage customs), aspects of political organization (e.g., local groups, political hierarchy), ritual, and religion. It provides a broad inventory of Nyanga material culture, and gives succinct references to basic techniques of agriculture and honey-harvesting. The epic also tries to account for the origin of certain institutions (cult of Lightning, fission of political entities, hunting taboos imposed on chiefs). It further provides a synopsis of basic Nyanga values. And finally, it permits us to enter the personal world of the narrator, who inserts many of his own reflections and meditations.

THE SYSTEM OF TRANSCRIPTION
I. *The Symbols Used in the Nyanga Text*

A. Vowels

	Degree of aperture
i̜, u̜	1st
i, u	2d
e, o	3d
a	4th

In the English translation we have not maintained this distinction; i is used to represent the Nyanga i̜ and i, u is used to represent the Nyanga u̜ and u.

B. Semivowels
  1. There are two front semivowels y:
        y corresponding to i̜ as in *iya:* to come
        ÿ corresponding to i as in *iÿa:* to kill
  2. There is only one back semivowel w.

C. Consonants
  The characters of the Roman alphabet are used with the following specifications:
  1. The nasal onset consonant cluster *ns* is represented as *nts*.
  2. The nasal palatal ja (I.P.A.) is represented as *ny*.
  3. The voiceless palatal fricative ʃ (I.P.A.) is represented as *sh*.
  4. The voiceless palatal affricate *tʃ* (I.P.A.) is represented as *c* (pronounced as in the English "church").

D. Tones
  high tone: ´   rising tone: ˇ
  low tone: no sign   falling tone: ^

E. Capital letter in the middle of a word, preceded or not by a hyphen or apostrophe, to indicate the beginning of a proper noun, for example, Bana-Muki̜ti̜ (those of Mukiti's group).

F. Apostrophe. Used to indicate elision of final syllable vowel or of the initial semivowel, or, in some cases both:
      wamaki̜nd'i̜binga for *wamaki̜ndá ibinga* (he had finished marrying) *kumbo'ĕrŭsi* for *kumbo wérŭsi* (downstream of the river) *mwi̜r'aní* for *mwi̜ra wani* (my friend)

G. Hyphen. Used to indicate the compounding of a bound morpheme and a word (e.g., *shé*-Mwindo: father of Mwindo) or the
reduplication of morphemes (e.g., *ikíákia*, to do often; lit., to do
and do, from *ikía*, to do).

II. Word Division in the Nyanga Text

The principles of word division followed in the transcription of the
Nyanga text are outlined in great detail in a forthcoming study by Mr.
Kahombo C. Mateene.[7] The nominal and verbal forms, the locative *hó*,
ko, *mo*, the possessive and demonstrative pronouns, the invariables,
such as *nti* (then), *ngí* (it is), *ntí* (it is not), *mbu* (that, saying that), the
associative particle *na* (and, with, etc.), and so on, are treated as words.

NOTES ABOUT THE TRANSLATION

We have tried to be as literal as possible, yet produce a readable text.
We often draw attention to an interpreted translation in the notes.
One of the greatest difficulties rested in the common occurrence of
what could be called a mixed form of discourse (direct and indirect).
A simple instance of this procedure is given in the following sentence:

> *básúbíe Mukítí mbu bó báshịmá, ǒngo Mukítí, múkinwa cábé, íyé
> wendaa kánonka . . . nti íyé ǒngo'nonkéngi bó.*

translated as:

> They answered Mukiti saying: we are satisfied, (you) Mukiti, because of
> your word; now you will go to win valuables . . . from now on you win
> them for us.

Literally the Nyanga sentence reads:

> They answered Mukiti that *they* were satisfied, *you* Mukiti, because of
> *your* word, now go to win valuables . . . from now on you win (them)
> for *them*.

It would have been simple to put this sentence completely in the form
of direct discourse by changing *bó báshịmá* into *bǎte* (we) *twashịmá*

---

7. Under the title "Nouvelles considérations sur la délimitation des mots dans une
langue bantoue," to be published in *Cahiers d'Etudes Africaines* (Paris), nos. 25, 26.

(we are satisfied) and *ŏngo'nonkéngi bó* into *ŏngo'tunonkéngi*. This grammatical procedure is surely inspired by euphemism on the part of the narrator who, in songs and in gestures, tends to identify himself very strongly with the hero, and yet, whenever he can, tries to conceal this fact. The narrator treats the dialogues both as a distant witness and as a fully involved participant. The element of euphemism involved in the usage of direct, indirect, and mixed forms of discourse was clearly revealed to me in a tale, where the narrator began a dialogue between the hero of his story with *é titá* (oh! my father), and then immediately corrected himself, interrupting the dialogue by *ishé kuti namênda kwishámbaka we* (my father . . .!—no—his father, so that I would not go to attribute him to myself [i.e., to compromise myself by saying *my* father]).

There are also many terse or figurative expressions that are difficult to translate exactly. A few examples:

> *bákíé mbu básisimuké . . .*, lit., when they woke up, and translated as "in fixing their attention," but it is difficult to decide whether the narrator wants to express the idea of "the next morning" or of "suddenness," as if they had been day-dreaming and had suddenly come back to reality.
>
> *wákárisha bana-cé biÿo bĭngí*, translated as "he had his people prepare much food," but the verb implies an order for preparing food to be used as a counterpresent.
>
> *cúngu búmĭnĭrengi aní kumongo . . . niseéngi na múmatema*, translated as "see how I am dancing, my back (shivering) . . . and my cheeks contain my laughing," but the text literally says "see how I am dancing on the back; and I am laughing in the cheeks." (For young men good dancing is determined by the movements of the shoulder blades; a "laughing in the cheeks" is a standard expression for strong but contained laughing which makes the cheeks swell.)

The vocabulary is exceptionally rich and precise; there are many poetic and figurative uses of words to which attention is frequently drawn in the notes. The Nyanga language is very much concerned with repetitions indicating place, relative time, and circumstance:

> "There was a river in which there was a pool and in that pool there was in it Mukiti, Master-of-the-pools. In his dwelling place in the pool (lit., where he was seated, established, located in the pool) Mukiti. . . ."
>
> "When the night had become daylight, in the morning. . . ."

"After the divers, swimmers, had been found, they took . . .; when they arrived at the pool . . . the swimmers entered into the pool, they asked. . . ."

Although these repetitious statements are cumbersome in reading, they are a typical expression of Nyanga thought patterns and have therefore been left as they are.

The square brackets in the translation refer to words that are in Nyanga but make the translated sentence cumbersome. The parentheses in the translation refer to words that are absent from Nyanga but are necessary for a better understanding of the translated text.

Note: Walikale territory is now called Zone Walikale, and Kivu Province is now called Kivu Region.

The Mwindo Epic

Long ago there was in a place a chief called Shemwindo.[1] That chief built a village called Tubondo, in the state of Ihimbi.[2] Shemwindo was born with a sister called Iyangura.[3] And in that village of Shemwindo

1. *mwamí/chief*: traditionally, the Nyanga have no paramount chief. They are politically organized into petty states, each ruled by a sacred chief. Each chiefdom is autonomous, but the rulers are often linked by the recognition of a common agnatic origin or by affinal and friendship ties, *shé-Mwindo*: a typical construction for a teknonymic name, *shé-* (his father) followed by the name of the child. The chief's name here already foreshadows the name of his son to be born.

2. *ubúngú/village*: concept refers to a fairly large village (some 75 to 100 people on the average) occupied by members of more than one kinship group, in opposition to *kantsari*, a hamlet. *kuTubondo*: the Nyanga frequently name their villages after a dominant phytogeographical aspect of the area where they are located, *kabondo* means little raphia palm tree. Raphia palms are extremely important in Nyanga technology (in basketry and plaiting and in the making of traps and snares, money). Village names and other place-names always occur in Nyanga in conjunction with a locative prefix, mostly *ku-* (cl. 17). *cŭo/state*: the generic concept with which the Nyanga designate the petty chiefdoms into which they are subdivided. This term is then followed by a connective and by the specific name of the chiefdom to which reference is made. *Ihímbí*: not a legendary place, but one of the most isolated regions of Nyanga country, located in the Kisimba administrative unit of Walikale territory. The people inhabiting this region are said to be Bahímbí, outstanding hunters of big game among whom the Pygmy cultural impact is very strong. Most Nyanga speak about this place as a region of mystery and danger.

3. *wabútwá ná/was born with*: the forms used here do not indicate that Shemwindo and his sister were twins, but clearly show that they were full siblings, *mwjsíábó/a sister*:

there were seven meeting places of his people.⁴ That chief Shemwindo married seven women.⁵ After Shemwindo had married those [his] seven wives, he summoned together all his people: the juniors and the seniors, advisors, the counselors, and the nobles.⁶ All those—he had them meet in council.⁷ When they were already in the assembly, Shemwindo sat down in the middle of them; he made an appeal, saying: "You my wives, the one who will bear a male child among you my seven wives, I will kill him/her; all of you must each time give birth to

---

mwįsį means girl; used with a possessive pronoun in the singular, it designates a daughter; used, as here, with a possessive pronoun in the plural, it refers to a sister, real or classificatory. *Iyangura*: a very uncommon personal name. Some of my informants related it to the verb "to arbitrate," meaning that she received this name because of her father's qualities as an arbiter; others tended to see a connection with the verb relating to the performance of twin-birth ceremonies. In this epic, Iyangura acts as a kind of arbiter in the conflict that opposes her brother, Shemwindo, to his son, Mwindo.

4. *ndushú/meeting places*: oval-shaped huts with two doors which serve as the meeting places for daily as well as ceremonial activities of the male members of a small, localized kinship unit. It is also used to designate that kinship group itself, *sirínda/seven*: the number here is purely symbolic; rarely, if ever, are there seven kinship units to the village in Nyanga society. In Nyanga thinking, seven is a perfect number; constant reference to it is made in some ethnohistorical traditions and in certain ritual practices. The number seven is frequently used throughout the epic: the chief has seven wives; he hurls his spear seven times; it rains for seven days; the hero asks for seven strokes of lightning, and so on.

5. *bomína/women*: the term *bakárí*, spouses, wives, is appropriate when all matrimonial prescriptions have been fulfilled. When speaking about a chief's wives, the term *bowé* would be more adequate.

6. The suggestion is made here that all people, young and old, male and female, officeholder and commoner, are called together. This is, of course, an unusual procedure, since normally only male *bakwákare* (seniors and officeholders) participate in such councils. It is to be noted that every petty chiefdom is a politically autonomous entity with its own apparatus of political officeholders who are basically of two categories: *barųsį*, members of the royal descent line, and *bakungú*, representatives of nonroyal descent groups.

7. *wárįa bó/he had them meet*: the verb *irįa* literally refers to the action of carrying, putting, bringing, *kįbú/council*: a large public meeting in which the members of various descent groups participate under the leadership of the chief to make political or jural decisions. The term *námá* used later on in the text concerns a secret discussion that may be held during such a public meeting before any major decisions are announced.

girls only."[8] Having made this interdiction, he threw himself hurriedly into the houses of the wives, then launched the sperm where his wives were. Among his wives there was a beloved-one and a despised-one. The despised-one had (her house) built next to the garbage heap and his other wives were in the clearing, in the middle of the village.[9] After a fixed number of days had elapsed, those [his] seven wives carried pregnancies, and (all) at the same time.[10]

Close to the village of Shemwindo there was a river in which there was a pool, and in this pool there was a water serpent, master of the unfathomable.[11] In his dwelling place, in the pool, Mukiti heard the news that downstream from him there was a chief who had a sister called Iyangura; she was always glistening (like dew) like sunrays because of beauty.[12] After Master Mukiti had heard the news of the beauty of that young woman Iyangura, he went in pursuance of her in

8. *mbu/saying*: invariable word used throughout the text to introduce a song, a state-ment, or a dialogue (in direct or indirect or mixed direct-indirect discourse). According to the context, *mbu* is not translated or is rendered as "that . . ." or "saying. . . ." *I will kill him/her*: Nyanga is ambiguous here; it is not clear from the forms used whether the chief plans to kill the mother or the child; to the audience, however, which is fully acquainted with many similar stories, it is clear that the chief is threatening the child.

9. The distinction between the beloved wife and the despised wife is currently made in many Nyanga tales; it is part of the tensions that exist in the polygamous house-hold. The distinction is not made verbally by the husband, but exists *de facto* and is also made in conversations among the co-wives and by outsiders. Here, the distinction is presented as a formal arrangement whereby the despised wife would live away from the others, near the garbage heap, near the uncleared boundary line of the village and the forest. This is not so in fact. The image of building a hut on the garbage heap is con-nected with a pun: *hírare*, garbage heap, and *nyírare*, general form for co-wife.

10. *ná/and*: this word basically means "and, with," but according to its many possible positions in the sentence, it can add rich shades of meaning to the general statement, such as to evoke the unexpected, the abnormal, and so on. The surprise lies here in the fact that all the wives are pregnant simultaneously and after so short a period of marriage.

11. *Mukíti*: this fabulous water serpent is said to live in deep pools, and is therefore called here *miné-márjba*, master of the pools with which the Nyanga identify mystery. Many tales deal with Mukiti, who is represented as a fairly mild creature (not a terror like the forest spirit Mpacá or the dragon Kirjmu), sometimes married to a human wife he has lured into the water. He is said to be the chief of the water.

12. *kwárjkángá/in his dwelling place*: locative expression based on the verb *irjka*, to be seated, to be located. It often occurs in the text where we have translated it as "in his dwelling place, in their homestead."

order to court her.[13] Mukiti reached Tubondo; Shemwindo accommodated him in a guesthouse.[14] When they were already in twilight, after having eaten dinner and (food), Mukiti said to Shemwindo: "You, my maternal uncle, I have arrived here where you are because of (this one) your sister Iyangura."[15] Shemwindo, having understood, gave Mukiti a black goat as a token of hospitality and, moreover, said to Mukiti that he would answer him tomorrow.[16] Mukiti said: "Yes, my dear father, I

13. *Muna-Mukítí/Master Mukiti*: the expression *muna/bana* generally means "of the species, group, subject of." The names of most descent groups are preceded by it. In tales it is often used to introduce the hero and seems to be close in meaning to Master, Ma'itre. *kikumi/young woman*: nubile girl, maiden, a concept that refers to the category of women who have passed the *kitásá* age level and are ready for marriage. In general, it stresses the role and position of women as marriage partners; men, e.g., refer to all married female members of their descent group as *kikumí*. *kámukóhe/in order to court her*: *ikóhe* actually stands for the discreet winking that is part of the secret courtship of the Nyanga.

14. *mwicumbi/in a guesthouse*: any house in which visitors are accommodated for the night can be called *icumbi*. Only important persons, e.g., elders of descent groups or political officeholders, have specially built, oval-shaped guesthouses. Accommodating visitors in a house and giving them food are considered to be the fundamental signs of hospitality, friendship, and generosity. Only after a full welcome has been expressed are the issues that led to the visit raised.

15. *jrengera/eat dinner*: technical term for the main evening meal eaten at about 6 P.M. The Nyanga also have a morning meal (*usimbiro*) and a late supper (*utóte*) which is consumed in strict privacy by husband and wife. The term (*biÿo*), food, is superfluous. It is interesting that Mukiti calls Shemwindo maternal uncle. There is no interpretation given in the text for this form of address. We can, however, conceive of a situation whereby Mukiti goes to marry his *musárá*, matrilateral cross-cousin, identifying the girl's brother with her father (common in some kinship nomenclatures of eastern Congo peoples). The Nyanga have ambivalent attitudes toward cross-cousin marriages: generally speaking, marriages between children of full siblings of opposite sex are not tolerated; in the classificatory sense, the more common form of cross-cousin marriage is between a man and his patrilateral cross-cousin (the opposite of what happens here). As so often happens, we have here, in Mukiti's words, a strange blend of direct and indirect discourse. Literally, Mukiti says: "You, his maternal uncle, it is the reason why he has arrived here where you are."

16. *wáshee . . . nceo/he gave as a token of hospitality*: *jshea*, with or without *nceo*, is a technical word, used for any gift of hospitality to a relative, to a jocular relative, or to a blood friend. It is different from sharing food with a stranger or an unimportant person. Stress is placed on the fact that the goat is black; black goats are rare. In the traditional system of matrimonial exchanges among the Nyanga, the goat was given to the future son-in-law as a form of consent. The action is somewhat shortened here, since the prospective parents-in-law generally reserve their definite answer for some time.

am satisfied."[17] When the night had become daylight, in the morning, Mukiti made himself like the anus of a snail in his dressing up; he was clothed with raphia bunches on the arms and on the legs, and with a belt (made) of bongo antelope, and he also carried an *isia*-crest on the head.[18] In their homestead, Shemwindo and his sister Iyangura also overstrained themselves in dressing up.[19] The moment Mukiti and Shemwindo saw each other, Mukiti said to his father-in-law. "I am astonished—since I arrived here, I have not yet encountered my sister."[20] Hearing that, Shemwindo assembled all his people, the counselors, and the nobles; he went with them into secret council.[21] Shemwindo said to his people: "(Our) sororal nephew has arrived in this (village) looking for my sister; and you then must answer him." The counselors and nobles, hearing that, agreed, saying: "It is befitting that you first present Iyangura to Mukiti." They passed with Iyangura before Mukiti. Mukiti, seeing the way in which Iyangura was bursting

17. *titá shé-karụo/my dear father*: lit., my father, master or possessor of the ladle. This is an honorific term much used by the Nyanga under the form of *nyakarụo* to refer to their wife or mother. The emphasis is on the ladle (*irụo*) that women use to stir the banana paste, and to the *mirúo*, ceremonial meal that accompanies the rituals celebrated at the birth of a child.

18. *búri kanyero kânkó/like the anus of a snail*: symbol of neatness, cleanliness. The idea of beauty is further enhanced by the belt made of bongo antelope, the symbol of beauty and greatness. The idea of festivity is rendered by the bunches of raphia fibers and the *ịsịa*-crest which the Nyanga wear in many of their dances. The *ịsịa*-crest consists either of part of an elephant tail or of whiskers of leopards and genets fixed into a little brass disc.

19. *bịmónya/overstrained themselves*: lit., *imóna* means to undergo an initiation (circumcision or initiation into an association) with the implication of the pains, strains, and difficulties it entails. The reflexive causative form of *imóna* used here stresses that they exposed themselves to such hardships.

20. *ishibé/his father-in-law*: this terminology conforms with the fact mentioned earlier that the girl's brother takes the position of the un-mentioned girl's father, *mubịtụ'ani/my sister*: as stated, Mukiti is marrying his matrilateral cross-cousin, who is known descriptively as *musárá*. As among other eastern Congo populations, a female cross-cousin is also known as sister in the system of terminology. In fact, the Nyanga severely criticize the few individuals who marry their cross-cousins by saying: You married your sister. There is strong emphasis here on various close kinship relationships, whereby Mukiti tries to prove by all means that he has kinship rights in the girl.

21. *námá/secret council*: a decision-making process in which Mukiti cannot participate. Again, it is not necessary for all to participate, but, by stressing total participation, the importance and unusual character of the affair are once more underlined.

with mature beauty, asked himself in (his) heart: "Now she is not the one (I expected to see); she is like a *ntsembe-tree*."[22] Iyangura, indeed, was dressed in two pieces of bark cloth imbued with red powder and *mbea*-oil.[23] Seeing each other, Mukiti and Iyangura darted against each other's chests; (they) greeted each other. Having greeted each other, Iyangura said to Mukiti: "Do you really love me, [you] Mukiti?" Mukiti told her: "Don't raise (your) voice anymore, [you] my wife; see how I am dancing, my back (shivering) like the raphia-tree larva, and my cheeks contain my laughing."[24] After Mukiti and Iyangura had seen each other in this manner, the counselors and nobles of Shemwindo answered Mukiti, saying: "We are satisfied, [you] Mukiti, because of your word; now you will go to win valuables; whether you win many, whether you win few, from now on you win them for us."[25] After Mukiti had been spoken to in that way, he returned home with

22. *búkókóbócáángé/was bursting with mature beauty*: the expression is difficult to translate; we have given it a reasonable interpretation. The expression is commonly used, particularly by men, to refer to the beauty of women. The verb *ikókóboka* literally signifies the bursting of nuts detaching themselves from the tree, but it connotes, at the same time, the idea of glitter, refulgence, very much like the French *éclat. Now she is not the one . . .*: current way of expressing great astonishment; the meaning conveyed is that the girl is much more beautiful than he had anticipated. She is therefore compared to the *ntsémbe-tree*, a tall, straight, very smooth tree that cannot be cut in the fields lest lightning strike the house where its wood is burned.

23. Women traditionally have two pieces of bark cloth hanging from their belts, one in the front and one in the back. Underneath, they wear a small piece of cloth (*mushúkú*) which covers the genitalia. Red ointment made from camwood or from red clay and castor oil is widely used.

24. *bókane múmakuba/darted against each other's chests*: this way of greeting is normal between related individuals. The narrator emphatically insists on the irresistible attraction between Mukiti and Iyangura, as if he wanted to excuse her marriage and her absence from the village where the hero is to be born. In order to prove his feelings, Mukiti makes what the Nyanga consider to be a forceful demonstration of love by dancing before Iyangura, the movements of his body reflecting the joyful undulations of the larvae found in a fallen raphia tree.

25. The specific amount of matrimonial goods to be given is not prescribed; this is normal because it is a cross-cousin marriage. The noticeable indifference and skepticism of the speakers are striking here. Their attitude owes partly to the fact that they know Mukiti to be a strong man; there is also the implication that from now on Mukiti is indebted to them.

soothed heart.[26] Returning home, they fixed him seven days for bringing the valuables.[27]

After Mukiti was home, he assembled his people (and) told them
that he was just back from courting, that he had been assigned nine
thousand, and a white goat, and a reddish one, and a black one, and one
for sacrifice, and one for the calabash, and one for the mother, and one
for the young men.[28] The counselors and the nobles, hearing that,
clapped their hands, saying to their lord that they were satisfied, that
they could not fail to find that payment of goods (enough), because this
maiden was not to be lost.[29] After the seven days were fulfilled, in the

26. *nti émutima wámámusįka/with soothed heart*: lit., it is that the heart climbs
down in him; the verb *įsįka* (to climb down, e.g., from a tree) is currently used to indicate relief of tension; "the heart is high" (*kwįyo*) means tension, anxiety. It is normal for
Mukiti to be unsure about the outcome of his request for three reasons. First, marriages
with matrilateral cross-cousins are unusual; second, Iyangura is of noble descent, and
girls of her rank among the Nyanga can only be married to spirits; third, Mukiti had not
secretly linked himself to his female cross-cousin by giving her a certain kind of present,
the meaning of which is unclear to her and the acceptance of which signifies her agreement. Let us, finally, point out that it is unusual for a man to go to ask for his cross-
cousin (or sister, as she is called); there is verbal symbolism involved in the request
made not for the girl but for a little calabash.

27. *bámuraa/they fixed him*: the verb *įrana* literally means to say good-bye and to
leave an oral will. The number of days fixed is purely symbolic.

28. *bihumbi mwendá/nine thousand*: i.e., nine thousand matrimonial goods (*béhe*)
or an amount of nine thousand measures of *butéá*-money (*byábutéá*), all simply to
say that an enormous amount of goods is requested. The different types of goats
specified bear on actual matrimonial practices; each has a well-defined destination.
The white goat is to be shared by the young men of the girl's descent group; the reddish
one goes to the girl's mother's descent group; the black one goes to the girl's mother;
the goat for sacrifice is to be distributed by the head of the girl's descent group
among all fifteen male and female members; the goat for the calabash (syn. with the
other one for the young men) is to be shared by all the male members of the girl's
descent group who supply her with chickens. The enumeration of goats is not complete;
among those mentioned, however, some are part of *ndįko* (the core group of marriage
payments), and others fit into the category of reciprocal gifts exchanged during the
course of married life. The usual procedure for arranging a marriage and the various,
gradual steps by which a legal marriage is insured are much more complicated than
suggested here.

29. *bákóngóta múmįne/clapped their hands*: this is one of the ways in which people
mark their agreement in important discussions. It can also be done by humming
(*nįnga*). *nyeré-kurwábó/their lord*: compound word, which literally means master-lord

morning, Mukiti took the marriage payments to go, and his people remained behind him; they went to Shemwindo's to give him the payments. On leaving his village, he went to spend the night in the village of the Baniyana.[30] The Baniyana gave him a ram as a token of hospitality. The Banamukiti and Mukiti himself slept in that village, being like a blister because of repletion.[31] In the morning, Mukiti woke up; he went to throw himself into the village of the Banamitandi; the Banamitandi gave Mukiti a goat as a token of hospitality; he spent the night there.[32] In the morning, he set out from one of the ways out (of the village) together with his people, (and) went to arrive at long last in the village of his fathers-in-law, in Tubondo, at Shemwindo's.[33] When they arrived in Tubondo, Shemwindo showed them a guesthouse to sleep in and also gave them a billy goat as a present of hospitality. In the late evening, Iyangura heated water for her husband; they went together to wash themselves.[34] Having finished washing themselves, they anointed

---

in a village (*ubúngú*) and is currently used to refer to a chief, to the head of a descent group; women also use it in addressing their husbands in order to flatter them.

30. *múmukomá-kóma/in the morning*: i.e., next morning. When the heroes in the epic set out on a trip or an exploration, they always do so in the early morning, *his people remained behind him*: this does not mean that the chief leads the line and that all the others follow but that the journey is made in his name, on his behalf; he is the greatest of them all. Again, it is unusual for the groom himself to take the payments to his wife's family unless he has no close relatives living. *Baniyana*: lit., the kinship group of the hundreds, of those who are very numerous; here, "the hundreds" refer to the bats. As mentioned later in the text, the bats are generally represented as the blacksmiths who "forge" (strengthen) the heroes.

31. *kihárábúté/ram*: this is a sign of exceptional hospitality; mutton is highly rated for its fat; moreover, sheep have a sacred character, whereas goats are used in profane contexts. *Bana-Mukíti*: all people who are following him and who are under his authority.

32. *Bana-Mitandi*: lit., the kinship group of the spider webs, which here stands for the spiders themselves. In tales, spiders appear as helpful creatures, makers of bridges that save the heroes.

33. *wísíca kwíkúra/he set out from one of the ways out*: lit., he put his own burden down at the way out of the village. A traditional Nyanga village had two *íkúra*. The village was fenced and had two entrances (one "upstream" and one "downstream") where connecting paths to other villages began; *íkúra* was the cleared space in front of the two gateways, but outside the fence, i.e., outside the village, *bishíbé/fathers-in-law*: all brothers and male agnatic parallel cousins of one's real father-in-law are terminologically identified with one's father-in-law.

34. *they went together to wash themselves*: it is customary for a woman to wash her lover's or husband's feet before going to bed.

themselves with red powder; they climbed into bed; Iyangura put a leg across her husband.[35] In the morning, there was a holiday.[36] Shemwindo assembled all his people; they sat together in a group. When all the Banashemwindo were grouped together, Mukiti came out with the marriage payments (and) placed them before his fathers-in-law. His fathers-in-law were very satisfied with them. They told him: "Well, you are a man, one who has his nails cut."[37] After they had completely laid hold of the marriage payments, the Banashemwindo told Mukiti to return to his village; they would conduct his wife to him.[38] Hearing this, Mukiti said: "Absolutely all is well; what would be bad would be to be deceived." He returned to his (village). When he was already in his village, Mukiti had his people prepare much food because he was having guests come. When Shemwindo, who had remained in his village, realized that Mukiti had been gone a day, in the morning, he set out to follow him; they went to conduct Iyangura.[39] While going, the attendants carried Iyangura, without (allowing her) foot to set on the ground,

35. It was also customary for a woman to anoint her husband or lover with red ointment and to rub some of it on the bed itself, so long as they did not have children, *wákinduca ná moké nwĭndí/put a leg across her husband*: one of the many euphemistic expressions used in speaking about sexual intercourse. It must be noted that sexual intercourse is permitted only after the girl has been conducted to her husband's village, and it is most unusual for a man to have sexual intercourse with his wife in her parents' village.

36. *mushibo/holiday*: a day of rest when nobody goes to work in the fields or forest. On the occasion of important initiations, sacrifices, deaths, or marriages of important individuals, such days of rest are publicly announced by the village headman or high political officials; a village or an entire chiefdom may be affected by such a prescribed holiday. Supernatural sanctions are said to await those who do not observe the prescriptions.

37. *Banashemwindo*: all the people placed under chief Shemwindo's authority. *wábŭme ukeráá byăra/a man, one who has his nails cut*: the son-in-law is twice praised for his strength, for his strong personality. The term *wábŭme*, a man, is used by the Nyanga for an adult male who has gone through many experiences, has much knowledge, and has achieved full social and ritual status in his society. To have one's nails cut means the same as saying that one cannot be stopped by anything, that one is able to overcome doubt and fear. In contradistinction, the expression evokes the image of the long-nailed, fear-inspiring Mpaca, small, old spirit of the forest.

38. *jhérúka*: the technical term for conducting a wife to her husband's village. The marriage sequences and proceedings are considerably simplified in this text.

39. The preparation of food is one of the principal ceremonies on all important occasions (birth, marriage, initiation, sacrifices, and so on) except funerary rites.

in mud, or in water.[40] When the attendants arrived with the (incoming) bride at Mukiti's, Mukiti showed them to a guesthouse; they sat down in it. They seized a rooster "to clean the teeth."[41] In this guesthouse they had Iyangura sit down on an *utebe*-stool.[42] When she was already seated, she took out the remainder of the banana paste from which she had had breakfast in her mother's house in their village.[43] She and her husband Mukiti ate it. When her husband had finished eating from that piece of paste, they had still more banana paste with taro leaves prepared for them. When the paste and the leaves were ready in the house, they told Mukiti to sit down on an *utebe*-stool; and they placed the paste between both (of them). When they were grouped like that, they told Iyangura to grasp a piece of paste in her right hand and make her husband eat it together with a portion of meat.[44] Iyangura took a piece of paste (from the dish); she had her husband eat it; and her husband took a piece of paste, and he too had his wife eat it.[45] After (both)

40. *ébahérúcj/the attendants*: a wife is conducted to her husband's village by a number of related women (paternal aunt, grandmother, brothers' wives, junior sisters). The men do not carry the bride, as suggested here, but they help her to cross a river or to go through mud.

41. The bride is not usually taken to a guesthouse, but to the house of her husband's mother. A rooster "to clean the teeth": beautiful expression not technical among the Nyanga clearly suggesting the poetic skill of the narrator. Once again it should be noted that a son-in-law does not normally give chickens to his wife's people; he receives chickens from them.

42. *utebe-stool*: Iyangura sitting on such a stool suggests the exceptional ceremonial circumstance. Normally women sit on a piece of wood or on a skin; the *utebe*-stool is sacred; women sit on it only when their hair is shaved at the end of the mourning period for a husband or son.

43. *múmwǎbó kurwábó/in her mother's house in their village*: typical construction with locative prefixes, connectives, and pronouns. The English translation renders precisely the ideas conveyed by this construction.

44. Emphasis is placed here on the ritual importance attached to the right, in general, and to the right hand, in particular, among the Nyanga.

45. Reference is made here to the final marriage rite whereby the husband and wife ceremonially feed each other. This, however, is done only when the bride is sexually pure; the rite described here is directly in contradiction with the sexual relations between Iyangura and Mukiti mentioned earlier, *nyényj/with a portion of meat*: lit., any ingredient (vegetables, sauce, fish, meat) added to the banana paste. Banana paste is the single most basic item in the Nyanga diet; great value is placed on meat (dried or fresh) which is absolutely necessary for a successful ceremonial meal.

husband and wife had finished eating the paste, the counselors of Mukiti gave Shemwindo a strong young steer as a gift of hospitality.[46]

After they had finished eating this young steer, they answered Mukiti, saying: "Don't make our child here, whom you have just married, into a woman in ragged, soiled clothing; don't make her into a servant to perform labor."[47] After they had said this, in the early morning right after awakening, they went, having been given seven bunches of *butea*-money as a departure gift by Mukiti.[48] When the bridal attendants arrived in Tubondo, they were very happy, along with their chief Shemwindo. Where Mukiti and his people and his wife Iyangura remained, he made a proclamation saying: "[You] all my people, if one day you see a man going downstream, then you (will) tear out his spinal column, you Banamaka, Banabirurumba, Banankomo, Banatubusa, and Banampongo; however, this path here which follows the flow of the river, (it) is the great path on which all people pass."[49] After he had passed this interdiction regarding these two paths, and while in [this] his village there lived his Shemwami called Kasiyembe, Mukiti told his big headman Kasiyembe: "You, go to dwell with my wife Iyan-

46. *kimása cénkambú/a strong young steer*: the Nyanga living in the rain forest have no cattle; they are surrounded by the cattle-owning inhabitants of the savannah highlands. The Nyanga also traditionally trace their origin to the pastoral Bunyoro (Uganda). The term *kímása* is used to designate a young male buffalo.

47. Advice of this type is currently given at the end of the marriage ceremony. The girl is then called *mwán'ịtụ́* (our child) by the members of her group in order to stress their collective sense of duty and responsibility. *nya-turịco, nya-mirémbe/a woman in ragged, soiled clothing*: lit., a mother of holes, a mother of hanging things; the form *nyá-* (mother of) has many specialized usages to show that a female individual has a special association with a given object, right, disease, child, activity, and so on.

48. *mianda/bunches*: a heap, a lot, not a special measure of money. The same term is used, e.g., for a bundle of firewood or a heap of leaves. The choice of words is always very precise and technical; gift-giving when the guests are leaving is called *ịkósóra*.

49. Mukiti addresses various species of fishes and crabs which are presented as kinship groups under his control. *You (will) tear out his spinal column*: you will beat him up. The spinal column is called "the bone of the back." The proclamation made by Mukiti results from a kind of premonition; it is of fundamental importance to the further intrigue of the epic. Mukiti already knows that the hero Mwindo will come through the water in search of his aunt Iyangura; he therefore places a taboo on the river; the path that runs along the water, however, is said to be a public road on which all are allowed to pass. This interdiction by Mukiti will provide the hero Mwindo with an initial set of battles to fight and to win.

gura at the borders of the pool; and I Mukiti shall from now on always reside here where all the dry leaves collect in flowing down, where all the fallen tree trunks are obstructed in the middle of the pool."[50]

Where Shemwindo lived in Tubondo, together with his wives and all his people, they were very famous [there]; his fame went here and there throughout the entire country.[51] When (many) days had passed that his wives had remained pregnant, one day six of his wives pulled through; they gave birth merely to female children.[52] One among them, the preferred-one, remained dragging herself along because of her pregnancy. When the preferred-one realized that her companions had already given birth, and that she remained with (her) pregnancy, she kept on complaining: "How terrible this is! It is only I who am persecuted by this pregnancy. What then shall I do? My companions, together with whom I carried the pregnancy at the same time, have already pulled through, and it is I who remain with it. What will come out of this pregnancy?"[53] After she had finished making these sad reflections, reawakening (from her thoughts) [where she was], at the

50. It is understood, although not explicitly mentioned in the text, that Mukiti is a sacred chief and Iyangura is his *mumbo*, or ritual wife, whose son is to be his successor. It explains why Iyangura lives separately from Mukiti in a hamlet of her own, under the supervision and protection of an officeholder called Shemwami (father of the chief). Reference is thus made to an extremely complex set of customs and practices relating to the position of the ritual wife. The personal name Kasiyembe is rare in Nyanga society. It is derived from a small reed pipe, which generally accompanies praise songs for the chiefs, *mutámbo/headman*: common generic term referring to the senior member of a descent group or to the head of a hamlet or village; Kasiyembe is the headman of the hamlet in which the chief's ritual wife lives. *And I Mukiti shall . . . pool*: a very beautiful and succinct description of how the Nyanga conceive of the pool as a dwelling place of the water spirit Mukiti.

51. *nkúrú/fame*: not to be confused with *nkúru* (turtle); this fame can be good or bad. The concept of fame, glory, reputation, often mentioned in the text, is to be distinguished from other recurrent concepts, such as *karamo* (Lat., *salus*), health, long life, safety; *maá* (Lat., *vis*), physical strength, force; *buingo* (Lat., *fortuna*), destiny.

52. *bjkokora/pulled through*: lit., *jkokora* means to pull a thing out in order to make it longer; to undo the knots; the image conveyed is that the women "unknotted" themselves. The Nyanga explanation of this metaphor is that, in giving birth to girls, the women conformed with their husband's prescriptions.

53. *narandwá na/I am persecuted by*: the verb *jranda* means to sew, to baste; thus the woman exclaims that she is "sewn" by the pregnancy, or that the pregnancy sticks to her.

door then there was already a bunch of firewood; she did not know from where it had come; lo! it was [her] child, the one that was inside the womb, who had just brought it.[54] After some time had passed, looking around in the house, there was already a jar of water; she did not know whence it had come; all by itself it had brought itself into the house. After some time had passed, raw *isusa*-vegetables also arrived there at the house. When the preferred-one saw it, she was much astonished; lo! it was the child in her womb who was performing all those wonderful things.[55]

When the inhabitants of the village saw that the preferred-one continued to drag on with (her) pregnancy in her house, they got used to sneering at her: "When then will this one also give birth?" Where the child was dwelling in the womb of its mother, it meditated to itself in the womb, saying that it could not come out from the underpart of the body of its mother, so that they might not make fun of it saying that it was the child of a woman; neither did it want to come out from the mouth of its mother, so that they might not make fun of it saying that it had been vomited like a bat.[56] When the pregnancy had already begun to be bitter, old midwives, wives of the counselors, arrived there; they arrived there when the preferred-one was already being troubled with (the pains of the) pregnancy.[57] Where the child was dwelling in the womb, it climbed up in the belly, it descended the limb, and it went (and) came out through the medius. The old midwives, seeing him wailing on the ground, were astonished, saying: "It's terrible; is the

54. The simple meaning of this passage: the woman suddenly wakes up from the sad dreams she has been having because of the birth delay; her eyes wander around the hut until they light on the object placed near the entrance by her unborn child.

55. To make the meal complete, the unborn child brings to its mother some vital supplies (water, firewood, vegetables), the daily collection of which usually causes much hardship for women, *tushjngishj/wonderful things*: in this category the Nyanga group the bad omens (*bihúnda*), the good omens (*myangiriro*), and the extraordinary happenings (*bjshjsharo*) such as these, which cannot be known in advance through various ominous signs.

56. It is a widespread belief that bats give birth to their young through the mouth by vomiting them.

57. *barjkj/midwives*: not a specialized category of women; the term refers to older women who stand in a certain kinship relationship to the young mother and who are well informed about the various procedures, prescriptions, and teachings connected with childbirth.

child now replacing its mother?"[58] When they saw him on the ground, they pointed at him asking: "What (kind of) child (is it)?" Some among the old midwives answered: "It's a male child." Some of the old midwives said that they should shout in the village place that a male child was born. Some refused, saying that no one should shout that it was a boy who had just been born, because when Shemwindo heard that a boy had been born, he would kill him. Where the counselors were sitting together with Shemwindo, they shouted, asking: "What child is born there?" The old midwives who were sitting in the house kept silent, without giving an answer. After the birth of the child, the midwives gave him the name Mwindo, because he was the (first) male child who followed only female children in [their] order of birth.[59]

In that house where the child had been born (that day), there was a cricket on the wall.[60] Where Shemwindo was staying, after he had asked what child was born and the midwives were unwilling to give him an answer, the cricket left the house where the child had been born and went to say to Shemwindo: "You, chief, a male child was born there (from where I came); his name is Mwindo; that is why those who are in that hut there have not answered you." When Shemwindo heard that his preferred-one had given birth to a boy, he took up [to go with it] his spear; he rubbed it on a whetstone; he sharpened it; he went with it where the child had been born (that day). The moment he prepared to throw it into the birth hut, the child shouted from where it was; it said: "May this spear end up (each time it is being thrown) at the bottom of the house pole; may it never end

58. *wahingá/replacing*: the verb *ihinga* designates the exchange of one object for another.

59. It is customary for midwives to inform the men in the men's house of the birth of a child and to reveal its sex by laughing in a special way. It is not normal for midwives to name the child immediately after its birth; the child usually receives a name from its grandfather on the third day after its birth. One of the midwives goes to "buy" the name from the men, who are united in the men's house, with some measures of *butéá*-money and an empty dish. The name Mwindo is given to a boy who is born in a family where there are only girls or to a girl who follows a number of boys. Several informants saw a relationship between the name Mwindo and the verb *iindo* (to fell trees or to eradicate). Mwindo is also the name of a spirit of the Nyanga pantheon.

60. *kitúndúkútú/cricket*: in tales, he is thought to bring bad omens and to divulge secrets.

up where these old midwives are seated here; may it neither arrive at
the place where my mother is."[61] Shemwindo threw the spear into the
house six times, each time reaching nothing but [at] the pole. When
the old midwives saw that extraordinary event they stormed out of the
house; they fled away, saying (to one another) that they should not go
to die there. When Shemwindo had become exhausted from running
back and forth with his spear and had completely failed to kill Mwindo,
he spoke to his counselors, saying that they should dig a grave in order
to throw Mwindo into it, because he did not want to see a male child.
When the counselors had heard the order of the lord of their village,
they did not disagree with him; they dug the grave.[62] When (the grave)
was finished, they went to fetch the child Mwindo; they carried him
(handling him); so they went to bury him in the grave.[63] Mwindo
howled within the grave, saying: "Oh, my father, this is (the death)
that you will die, (but) first you will suffer many sorrows."[64] While
Shemwindo was hearing the sound of the Little Castaway, he scolded
his people, telling (them) to cover the grave right away.[65] His people
went to fetch fallen plantain stems; they placed them above him and
above the plantains they heaped much soil.[66] Lo! at his birth, at that
very moment, Mwindo was born with a *conga*-scepter, holding it in

61. *irungú/birth hut*: not a specially built hut, but any hut where an as yet unnamed
child resides, *ndúí/house pole*: middle pole of the hut which sustains the roof; it is said to
be the dwelling place of the tutelary spirit of the house; children must not sit near it.

62. *kabúrí/grave*: rare use of a Swahili word.

63. *bámubétábeta/they carried him (handling him)*: the verb means to lull to sleep in
the arms, but here the narrator simply suggests the way in which Mwindo is being carried and insists that Mwindo is really a small child, whatever his amazing feats are going
to be. *ikísa*: specialized term for ceremonial burial.

64. *rwâkwí . . ./this is (the death) . . .*: the word death is not mentioned, of course,
and that makes the way in which the threat is uttered remarkable; but the verbal prefix
used leaves no doubt in the Nyanga mind that reference to death, misfortune, is
intended. The verb *ikwá* has many shades of meaning in the text, ranging from to die in
the physical sense to suffering, diminution of status, excessive emotional experience,
and weakening or loss of life force.

65. *ékikoé/the sound*: only the distinctive sound or voice, *kátáwá/the Little Castaway*: the epithet is not used again in the epic; the term is currently applied to the children of a despised wife, implying neglect and rejection by the father.

66. *mitámbá/fallen plantain stems*: technical term applied to any kind of cut or
fallen banana tree.

his right hand.[67] He was also born with an adze, holding it in his left hand.[68] He was also born with a little bag of the spirit of Kahombo, wearing it slung across his back on the left side; in that little bag there was a long rope (within it).[69] Mwindo was born laughing and also speaking.[70]

When the day had ended, those who were sitting outdoors, seeing that where Mwindo had been thrown away [earlier in the day] there was light as though the sun were shining there, went to tell the men (about it) and the (latter) also arrived (there); they saw the place; they could not (bear to) stay a moment "which is long as what?" because the great heat, which was like fire, burned them.[71] Each time they did (as follows): as [this] one passed by, he cast his eyes there and proceeded on.[72] When they already were in the first vigil, when all the people were already

---

67. This passage in which the attributes of the hero at birth are described is the only one in the entire epic mentioned out of context by the narrator. *conga-scepter*: a flyswatter made from a buffalo tail or from the hairy tail of certain species of antelopes. The Nyanga attach great ceremonial and magic importance to these tails, which are carried, e.g., in the *kiowa* possession dances. The *conga*-scepter is the single most important attribute of Mwindo: throughout the epic it helps him to fly through the air, to kill, to destroy, to advise; it is the material symbol of the hero's force (physical and mental).

68. *mbasi/adze*: used by children to cut shrubs and small trees; also used to sculpture dishes and pestles, for harvesting honey, and so on. Serves as an emblem of the *bitumbu*, individuals who have the traditional right to organize a cycle of circumcisions and to perform masked dances while carrying the adze.

69. *kakú/little bag*: made from raphia fibers and used by men as a shoulder bag for carrying food, small tools, tobacco. It is also part of the cult objects hung in the shrine of the female spirit Kahombo. Kahombo is a spirit of good fortune and the bag stands here as a symbol of the good fortune with which the hero is born, *murí/a rope*: lit., a liana; here it is a kind of magic line by means of which the hero will later communicate with his paternal aunt.

70. It is unusual for the hero's speaking and laughing capabilities to be accented. If the hero were an animal, the two gifts would deserve special mention. The hero is human, and it is revealed later in the text that he likes to talk and boast excessively, two habits the Nyanga criticize constantly. Mwindo's epithet is *Kábútwa-kénda* (the Little-one-just-born-he-walked). For the narrator, and for the auditors, there is clearly something humorous about stressing two activities (laughing, talking) that, if practiced excessively, are subject to severe criticism.

71. *kashángí kárehyání/a moment "which is long as what?"*: current expression to say a very short period of time, a moment that has no length.

72. *wásúsa éméso/he cast his eyes*: the verb normally used is *isunda; isúsa*, which is employed here, means to plant a knife in the meat.

asleep, Mwindo got out of the grave; he went to sneak into the house of his mother.[73] As Mwindo was wailing in the house of his mother, (and) when where he was sitting Shemwindo began to hear the way in which the child was wailing in the house of the preferred-one, he was very much astonished, saying: "This time what was never seen is seen (for the first time); again a child cries in that house. Has my wife just given birth to another child?"[74] Shemwindo died of indecision (whether or not) to stand up, because of fear. Owing to his virile impetus, Shemwindo stood up; he went into the house of his wife, the house of the preferred-one, slithering like a snake, without letting his steps be noisy. He arrived at the hut; he peeked (through the open door), casting an eye into the house; he saw the child sleeping on the floor; he entered the hut; he questioned his wife, saying: "Where does this child come from again; did you leave another one in the womb to whom you have given birth again?" His wife replied to him: "This is Mwindo inside here."[75] Where Mwindo was sitting on the ground, he kept silent. Shemwindo, witnessing this marvelous event, his mouth itched (to speak) (but) he left the house without having retorted another word.[76] Where he went, he went to wake up the counselors. Arriving there, he told them: "What is there (behind me), is what is there; it is astounding."[77] He told them also: "Tomorrow, when the sky will have become day, then you will go to cut a piece from the trunk of a tree; you will carve in it a husk for a drum; you will then put the hide of a *mukaka*-antelope in the river to soften."[78] When the sky had become

73. *mahombekerera/first vigil*: this is a precise moment in the division of day and night as conceived by the Nyanga; it is the time when the men have left the meeting-house, when all the house doors are closed, but when not everybody has gone to sleep.

74. Difficult construction; the opposition is centered in *muri ína* (in the house of his mother) and *kwárikángá* (in the house where the boy's father was sitting).

75. *kantsóka/like a snake*: the prefix *ka* has the fairly rare meaning here of "in the manner of, like."

76. *kanangano/marvelous event*: lit., something that tells a tale.

77. Expressions similar to "what is there is what is there" are used frequently in daily speech to refer to extraordinary events.

78. *muhoró/husk*: the term stands for the hollowed, wooden frame of a drum before the membrane has been attached to it. The wooden frame and the completed drum itself are objects to which many prescriptions are linked. The Nyanga distinguish according to size and sound three types of drums (*mukíntsá, kioma,* and *kandûndú*) which are normally kept by the elder of a kinship group in the men's meetinghouse or in a shrine. *mukaka-antelope*: the membranes of drums are made from elephant ears and from the hides of several types of antelope, including the waterbuck referred to here.

day, all the people assembled together [calling one another]; they went to see Mwindo in the house of his mother. Mwindo was devoured by the many longing eyes. After they had looked at him, the counselors went to the forest to cut a piece of wood for the husk of the drum.[79] They arrived in the forest; they cut it (the piece of wood); they returned with it to the village. Arriving in the village, they carved the wood; they hollowed it out so that it became a husk. When the husk was finished, they went again to fetch Mwindo; they carried him (handling him); they stuck him into the husk of the drum. Mwindo said: "This time, my father has no mercy; what! a small baby is willingly maltreated!"[80] The Banashemwindo went to get the hide for the drum; they glued it on top of the drum; they covered it (the drum) with it.[81] When Shemwindo had seen how his son had been laid in the drum, he declared to all his people that he wanted two expert divers, swimmers, to go [the next day] and throw this drum into the pool where nothing moves.[82] After the divers, swimmers, had been found, they picked up the drum; all the people abandoned the village; they went to throw Mwindo. When they arrived at the pool where nothing moves, the swimmers with the drum entered the pool, swimming in the river. When they arrived in the middle of the pool, they asked in a loud voice: "Shall we drop him here?" All those who were sitting on the edge of the river answered "Yes," all saying together: "It is there, so that you will not be the cause of his return."[83] They released the drum in the middle of the pool; it sank into the depths.[84] The waves made rings above

79. *báhíta/they went*: *ihíta* is a technical term that simultaneously means two things: to go down the hill (traditionally all Nyanga villages are located toward the tops of the hills) and to leave the village in order to do some kind of work (cultivation, trapping, fishing) in the forest. *mundụra/forest*: the part of the forest close to the village.

80. *busará/forest*: the general term for forest, as opposed to village (*mbúka*); the forest is then differentiated into various categories according to type of vegetation, proximity or distance from the village, types of activities pursued in it. *kabóntsó-bóntso/ small baby*: a few days or weeks old. This is, of course, a humorous note, but throughout the epic the hero continues to insist on his youth and smallness.

81. The verbs *ịkanga* and *ibamba* are technical for fixing the membrane of the drum with pegs and laces.

82. *bịndamị/divers*: the fishing technique of diving with nets is known in some areas of Nyanga country.

83. Note that the swimmers go to throw the drum into a pool, which is said to be a place of danger and the abode of Mukiti.

84. *ékumunda/into the depths*: lit., inside the pool, i.e., it was submerged.

the place where the drum had entered. After the swimmers had thrown him into the pool, they returned to the shore. Shemwindo was very pleased with them: "You have performed (good) work!" He gave each swimmer a maiden; thus those two got married because of (receiving) a gift for their labor.[85] That day, when Mwindo was thrown away, earth and heaven joined together because of the heavy rain; it rained for seven days; hailing left the earth no more; that rain brought much famine in Tubondo.[86]

After they had thrown Mwindo away, they returned to Tubondo. When they arrived in the village, Shemwindo threatened his wife Nyamwindo, saying: "Don't shed tears weeping for your son; if you weep, I shall make you follow up where your son has been thrown away." That very day, Nyamwindo turned into the despised-one.[87] Unable to weep, Nyamwindo went on merely sobbing—not a little tear of weeping!

Where Mwindo dwelt in the pool where he had been thrown away, when he was in the water on the sand, he moaned inside the drum; he stuck his head to the drum; he listened attentively; he said: "I, to go downstream the river, and this without having warned my father and all his people who have thrown me away so that they hear the sound

85. *uhémbo/gift*: not just any gift, but a kind of prize, of award, given for special achievements; e.g., in this category of gifts fall the presents given to an outstanding dancer or to people who perform clearing work in one's banana grove. There are many occasions on which chiefs give women as "presents" to officeholders, to followers, or to persons who perform special jobs for them.

86. *ÿéca ná mitabero irínda ikenga/it rained for seven days*: lit., there passed seven days it rains continually (habitually). *mutabero/day*: literally means a period of work, an order of work. At this early stage of the epic, several basic elements that set the heroic model are already present. Mwindo is born against the will of the chief (not of a virgin, but of the chief's favorite wife). He is born in an abnormal way (longer period of gestation and through mother's medius by his own will). From birth on he has extraordinary gifts (walking, laughing, talking) and magical powers (particularly *conga*-scepter) at his disposal which will permit him to cope successfully with his enemies. He is self-conscious and self-assertive. Not being wanted, he is thrown away: his fate affects the cosmic order (rain, hail, famine). His force and his will to overcome his enemies are still weak at this stage of the epic, but gradually increase to reach the level of absolute superiority.

87. *Nyamwindo*: Mwindo's mother; teknonymic name, *nya-kashómbé/despised-one*: the wife is not formally declared to be disgraced, but it is a *de facto* condition, which is declared a disgrace by the woman concerned.

of my voice—well then, I am not Mwindo."[88] Where the drum was in the water on the sand, it arose all alone to the surface of the water. When the drum was at the surface of the pool—in its middle—it remained there; it did not go down the river; neither did it go up (the river).

From Tubondo, from the village where the people dwelt, came a row of maidens; they went to draw water from the river at the wading place.[89] Arriving at the river, as soon as they cast their eyes toward the middle of the pool, they saw the drum on the surface of the water, which was turning around there; they said inquiringly to one another: "Companions, we have dazzling apparitions; lo! the drum that was thrown with Mwindo—there it is!" Where Mwindo dwelt inside the drum in the pool, he said: "If I abstain from singing while these maidens are still here drawing water from the river, then I shall not have anybody who will bring the news to the village where my father is in Tubondo."[90] While the maidens were in the act of drawing water and still had their attention fixed there toward the drum, Mwindo, where he dwelt in the drum in the pool, threw sweet words into his mouth; he sang:[91]

88. *wáhúrúkírire/he listened attentively*: the verb specifically applies to the way in which the children by different wives of the same man eavesdrop upon the conversations of the other women for their mother.

89. *hítúkúriro/wading place*: the wading place is not, in fact, meant here, but rather a spot a little upstream from the wading place where women draw water; between both spots is a bathing place. In the preceding passage, and in many others throughout the text, the Nyanga obsession for place designation is striking. The religious effort to be very precise in assigning spatial relationships is one of the most singularly typical traits of Nyanga thinking, but, of course, it makes translations cumbersome.

90. *bana-kítú/companions*: lit., members of our . . . (chiefdom, kinship group); people who interact with one another. The precision and the richness of the terms used are once more revealed here, e.g., "we have dazzling apparitions (*ihúmánana*, to be witness of something extraordinary, to have the apparition of a spirit or of the spirit of a paternal aunt in a dream); "said inquiringly to one another" (*bábúsá-nya*, the effect is achieved here by the suffix-*nya*). In none of the hundreds of tales that I collected in all corners of Nyanga country did I encounter such richness, diversity, and precision of language, such poetic quality and style.

91. *énderí/sweet words*: lit., sweet grains; the terms can also be used for an oral will left by a dying father or for a prophetic statement. In the song that follows, Mwindo forecasts that he will find his paternal aunt and that he will overcome his father and his father's counselors.

Scribe, move on![92]
I am saying farewell to Shemwindo!
I am saying farewell to Shemwindo!
I shall die, oh! Bira![93]
My little father threw me into the drum!
I shall die, Mwindo!
The counselors abandoned Shemwindo;
The counselors will become dried leaves.[94]
The counselors of Shemwindo,
The counselors of Shemwindo,
The counselors have failed (in their) counseling!
My little father, little Shemwindo,
My little father threw me into the drum
I shall not die, whereas (that) little-one will survive![95]
The little-one is joining Iyangura,
The little-one is joining Iyangura,
Iyangura, the sister of Shemwindo.[96]

92. *Karánj/scribe*: a Swahili word. This exclamation made by the narrator must be considered in the light of the general circumstances under which he sang his epic. We were sitting with him and patiently writing down the words that he sang and chanted. The encouragement is directed toward the assistant singers and the percussionists as much as toward myself. At the very start of a song or dance, there is in a moment of disorganization, of hesitation, a searching for exact rhythms and words. During such moments, even in important initiatory situations, all kinds of improvised sentences may be sung.

93. *Bjra*: under this term the Nyanga classify all those who are not of their culture, particularly the uncircumcised Hunde. There is raillery and challenge in this verse. Mwindo, in a somewhat covert way, says: "Do you, weaklings, think that I shall die now?" The tones used in the songs are not always regular ones; they are influenced by the music and singing. Thus Bjra is indicated here with two low tones, whereas normally it is pronounced Bjrá, with a rising and a low tone.

94. *Katitá/my little father*: the *ka-* prefix used here may have a diminutive or pejorative meaning. It is also to be noted, however, that Mwindo, who has a baby's stature, tends to view all others in terms of his own size. *ntsêkwá/I shall die*: difficult to interpret. It may be understood in three ways: "I shall die"; "shall I die"; or, if one accepts an eventual omission of *mbu*, "thinking that I shall die." The last interpretation makes the text more comprehensible: "My little father threw me into the drum! (thinking that) I shall die."

95. Difficult verse, which can be rightly understood only if we accept two different subjects: I shall not die (*ntákwí*) and he (my father) that little-one survive! (*kárami; ka-*bearing on *katitá*).

96. *Kábingúrá/the little-one is joining*: the prefix *ka-* bears on Mwindo himself. He has already called himself a little baby (*kabóntsóbóntso*) and he continues to refer to himself with this diminutive prefix (*ka-*).

When the girls heard the way in which Mwindo was singing in the drum in the pool, they climbed up to the village, running and rushing, after they had left the water jars at the river, behind (them), in disarray.[97] When they arrived within the inhabited area, the men, seeing them appear at the outskirts running and rushing, took their spears and went, believing that they were being chased by a wild beast.[98] Seeing the spears, the maidens beseeched their fathers: "Hold it! We are going to bring the news to you of how the drum that you threw into the pool has stayed; it is singing: 'The counselors of Shemwindo, the counselors have failed in (their) counseling; the counselors will become dried leaves.'" When he heard that, Shemwindo told the girls that they were lying: "What! the drum that we had thrown away [yesterday] into the pool arose again!" The maidens assented (to it): "Mwindo is still alive." They had seen him with (their own) eyes, and he (really) was still alive. When Shemwindo heard that, he assembled (again) all his people; the village remained empty; everybody deserted (the village) for the river carrying spears, arrows, and fire (torches).[99]

Where Mwindo dwelt in the river, after he had seen the way in which the maidens had cleared (the river) for the village, he also stopped (his) singing for a while; he said that he would sing again when the people arrived, because these girls had just witnessed his

97. *kumbúka/to the village*: the term *mbúka*, village has many interesting usages, which are revealed later in the text. Joined to the locative prefix *ha-* (*hámbúka*), it stands in opposition to *múnumba* and means outside, outdoors, as against inside, in the house, indoors. Joined to the locative prefix *ku-* it may designate two different things according to the context of oppositions in which it is used. If opposed to *kubusará* (the forest), it means "the village, the immediate surroundings of the village"; if opposed to *kwirúngá* (the craters of the volcanoes said to be the domain of the spirits), it means "the world inhabited by mankind."

98. *kihuká/wild beast*: the term can either indicate any kind of animal not raised in the village or specifically refer to some animals thought to be very dangerous, like the leopard and gorilla.

99. *tŏto/hold it*: an onomatopoeia meaning don't!; for mercy's sake! The young maidens seem to be somewhat on Mwindo's side, and, later on, they are found among his followers, *éngoma twaréré twatáá ÿo/the drum that we had thrown away yesterday*: typical way of expressing a recent past, literally means: the drum, we have slept we have thrown it away. *Carrying spears*: although the people know that the girls speak about Mwindo, they nevertheless make preparations, as if going to a big fight or as if setting out on a longer hunting expedition.

astonishing deed. All the people of the village, children and youngsters, old people and young men, women, when they arrived at the
river, seeing the drum in the middle of the pool, grouped together
looking attentively at the drum. When Mwindo noticed them waiting
in a group on the shore (of the river), he threw sweet words into (his)
mouth; he sang:[100]

> I am saying farewell to Shemwindo;
> I shall die, oh Bira!
> The counselors abandoned Shemwindo.
> Scribe, move on!
> The counselors will turn into dried leaves.
> What will die and what will be safe
> Are going to encounter Iyangura.[101]

When Mwindo had finished singing like that, saying farewell to his
father and to all the Banashemwindo, the drum sank into the pool; the
waves made rings at the surface. Where Shemwindo and his people
were standing on the shore, they were very perplexed; they nodded
their heads, saying: "How terrible it is! Will some day then be born
what is never being born?"[102] After they had witnessed this extraordinary event, they returned to the village Tubondo.

Where Mwindo headed inside the water, he went upstream; he
went to the river's source, at Kinkunduri's, to begin it.[103] When he

100. *bámatécá/waiting in a group*: *itéca* literally means to have somebody prepare
food (which implies that one is waiting to get it). The narrator describes these people as
if they were waiting there while food was being cooked for them.

101. *Kâkwí na Kárami/what will die and what will be safe*: Mwindo is speaking
about himself, of course, giving himself the epithets of Life (*Káramo*) and Death (*Kokú*).
The translation of *ka-* as a neuter form "*What will* . . ." is justified when the usage of this
prefix is examined in an expression like *káriho* (what lives, what is alive). When a
woman has a very difficult childbirth, the midwives say: "There will not come out what
is alive (*káriho*)."

102. *cásúmá/terrible*: the verb *isúma* is used whenever there are formidable physical, moral, or intellectual difficulties present.

103. *he went upstream*: the passage could imply two things: either that Mwindo had
been thrown into the river where Mukiti did not live, so he was now traveling upstream
to the source of another river where Mukiti had his dwelling place; or that the river into
which Mwindo had been thrown consisted of two levels: an upper one, through which
the hero could freely move, and a lower, or even subterranean one, which was the realm
of Mukiti and his allies. It was in this lower level that Mwindo would encounter many

arrived at Kinkunduri's, he lodged there; he said that he was joining Iyangura, his paternal aunt, there, whither she had gone; the news had been given him by Kahungu.[104] He began the trip; he joined his aunt Iyangura downstream; he sang:

Mungai, get out of my way!
For Ikukuhi shall I go out of the way?
You are impotent against Mwindo,
Mwindo is the Little-one just-born-he-walked.
I am going to meet Iyangura.
For Kabusa, shall I go out of the way?
You are helpless against Mwindo,
For Mwindo is the Little-one-just-born-he-walked.
Canta, get out of my way!
Canta, you are impotent against Mwindo.
I am going to encounter Iyangura, my aunt.
For Mutaka shall I go out of the way?
You are helpless against Mwindo!
I am going to meet Iyangura, my aunt.
For Kitoru shall I get out of my way?
You see, I am going to encounter Iyangura, my aunt.
I stated that:
For Mushenge shall I get out of my way?
You are impotent against Mwindo!
See, I am going to encounter Iyangura, my aunt,
Iyangura, sister of Shemwindo.
For Nyarui, shall I get out of my way?
Whereas Mwindo is the Little-one-just-born-he-has-
    walked.

---

difficulties. An interesting ritual concept is also linked with this passage. For the Nyanga, all bad things go downstream with the river. The frequent ablution ceremonies are held successively at different, but adjacent, spots along the river; the second ablution is always made a little farther upstream from the first, and so on. When the seventh and last stage of ablutions is completed, purity is achieved. In the pages that follow the hero encounters greater and greater obstacles during the river travel. In Nyanga thinking, this can happen logically only when he goes downstream (implying greater and greater accumulation of dirt and of inimical forces). *Kinkunduri*: the name for a species of crab found near river sources.

104. *Kahúngú*: a hawk, which, like the crowned eagle, often figures in tales as a friendly messenger.

I am going to encounter Iyangura, my aunt,
Sister of Shemwindo.
For Cayo shall I get out of my way?
You see, I am going to encounter Iyangura, my aunt,
Sister of Shemwindo.
Look! You are impotent against Mwindo,
Mwindo the Little-one-just-born-he-walked.
He who will go up against me, it is he who will die on the
    way.[105]

Each time Mwindo arrived in a place where an aquatic animal was, he said that it should get out of the way for him, that they were powerless against him, that he was going to his aunt Iyangura. When Mwindo arrived at Cayo's, he spent the night there; in the morning he went right after awakening; he sang:

> For Ntsuka shall I go out of the way?
> You see that I am going to encounter Iyangura.
> You see that you are powerless against Mwindo.
> Mwindo is the Little-one-just-born-he-walked.
> For Kirurumba shall I go out of the way?
> You see that I am going to encounter Aunt Iyangura.
> You see that you are powerless against Mwindo,
> For Mwindo is the Little-one-just-born-he-walked.
> For Mushomwa shall I go out of the way?
> You see I am going to encounter Aunt Iyangura.
> You see that you are powerless against Mwindo.
> For Mwindo is the Little-one-just-born-he-has-walked.

---

105. Several species of fishes and crabs, such as Mungai, Ikukuhi, Kabusa, Canta, Mutaka, Kitoru, Mushenge, Nyarui, Cayo, are mentioned in this song. They are all personifications of ugliness and hatred and considered to be allies of Mukiti. The names of these fishes remind the Nyanga of certain verbal forms that connote the idea of evil, *utúkocé/you are impotent/you are helpless*: negative of verb *ikoca*, to be able, to have the power, to have the capacity, to realize something. Mwindo often utters this expression to convey the idea that he alone is the hero. *Kábútwa-kénda/the Little-one-just-born-he-walked*: lit., little thing that was born, it walked. This is Mwindo's single most important epithet; the epithet is also found in tales as a name for extraordinary individuals. *Narimbura mbu/I stated that*: the narrator puts himself in the position of Mwindo; there are other instances in the text of this identification between Mwindo and the narrator, *ngí wakwírí muntse/it is he who will die on the way*: i.e., he will die lonely and abandoned.

Musoka, the junior sister of Mukiti, had gone to live upstream from Mukiti:[106]

> For Musoka shall I go out of the way?
> You are powerless against Mwindo
> Mwindo is the Little-one-just-born-he-has-walked.

When Musoka saw Mwindo arriving at her place, she sent an envoy to Mukiti to say that there was a person there where she was, at Musoka's, who was in the act of joining Iyangura. The envoy ran quickly to where Mukiti was; he arrived there (and) gave the news: "There is a person back there; he is in the act of joining Iyangura." Mukiti replied to that envoy that he should tell Musoka that that man should not pass beyond her place; "If not, why would I have placed her there?" That envoy arrived at Musoka's; he announced the news of how he had been spoken to by Mukiti. Musoka kept on forbidding Mwindo like that, without knowing that he was a child of Mukiti's wife, Iyangura. Musoka replied to Mwindo, saying: "Mukiti refuses to let you pass; so it is your manhood that will permit you to pass; I here, Musoka, I am placing barriers here; you will not find a trail to pass on." Mwindo answered her, softening his voice: "I, Mwindo, never am I forbidden (to pass on) a trail; I will thrust through there where you are blocking." Mwindo hearing this pulled himself together; he left the water above (him); he dug inside the sand; and he went to appear in between Musoka and Mukiti. After Mwindo had passed Musoka, having broken through the dam of Musoka, he praised himself: "Here I am, the Little-one-just-born-he-walked; one never points a finger at me." When Musoka saw him anew downstream, she touched (her) chin, saying: "How then has this tough one here gotten through? If he had passed above (me) I would have seen his shadow; if he had passed below (me), I would have heard the sound of his feet."[107] Musoka complained a lot saying that she would be scolded by Mukiti because she (had) let somebody pass.

106. Further enumeration of fishes and crabs, the personified allies of Mukiti, whose names evoke the idea of evil and hatred, e.g., *ntsúká*/vb. *isúku*, to frown in anger; *mushómwá*/vb. *ishómbwa*, to hate. Musóka, represented here as the junior sister of Mukiti, is a female water spirit for which the Nyanga have a special cult.

107. *one never points a finger at me*: i.e., nobody ever argues with me, nobody ever taunts me. *She touched her chin*: to express astonishment.

After Mwindo had passed Musoka, he began a journey to go to Mukiti's; he sang:

> In Mukiti's, in Mariba's dwelling place![108]
> For Mukiti shall I get out of my way?
> You see I am going to encounter Iyangura,
> Iyangura, sister of Shemwindo.
> Mukiti, you are powerless against Mwindo.
> Mwindo is the Little-one-just-born-he-walked.

When Mukiti in his dwelling place heard (this), he moved, asking who had just mentioned his wife. He shook heaven and earth; the whole pool moved. Mwindo on his side said: "This time we shall (get to) know each other today, we with Mukiti; (for) I Mwindo never fear an insolent child, so long as I have not measured myself against him."[109] When Mwindo heard that, he said: "This time, the husband of (my) aunt is lying; it is I Mwindo who am being forbidden the road to (my) aunt!" Mwindo pulled himself together; he went to appear at the knot where Mukiti was coiled up. When Mukiti saw him, he said: "This time it is not the one (whom I expected to see); he surpasses (expectation)!" He asked: "Who are you?" Mwindo referred to himself saying that he was Mwindo, the Little-one-just-born-he-walked, child of Iyangura. Mukiti said to Mwindo: "How then?" Mwindo answered him saying that he was going to encounter his paternal aunt Iyangura. Hearing that, Mukiti said to Mwindo: "You are lying; here never anybody passes, who would have crossed over these logs and dried leaves; so, then, you never go to sleep thinking! You alone are (the man) who in spite of all will (be able to) pass here where I am!" While Mukiti and Mwindo were still talking to each other like that, maidens went from Iyangura's place to draw water; at Mukiti's place, there it was that the water hole was. As soon as the maidens witnessed the way in which Mwindo constantly mentioned Iyangura saying (she was his) aunt, they ran to Iyangura; they arrived there (and) said to Iyangura: "Over there, where your husband Mukiti is, there is a little man saying that Mukiti should release him, that he is Mwindo, that he is going to

---

108. *Mariba*: lit., pool; Mukiti receives as an epithet the name of the place where he is thought to dwell.

109. *kitaba/an insolent child*: lit., a fat, indolent boy, spoiled and without energy.

encounter Iyangura, his paternal aunt." When Iyangura heard that news, she said: "Lo! that is my child, let me first go to where he is." Iyangura climbed up the slope; she went to appear at the water hole; she looked to the river that she first might see the man who was mentioning that she was Iyangura. As soon as Mwindo in his place saw his paternal aunt coming to see him, he sang:

> I am suffering much, Mwindo.
> I will die, Mwindo.

While his aunt Iyangura was then descending (the slope), he went on singing looking in the direction from which his aunt was coming.

> Aunt Iyangura,
> Mukiti has forbidden me the road.
> I am going to meet Aunt Iyangura,
> I am going to encounter Iyangura,
> Sister of Shemwindo.
> For Mukiti shall I go out of the way?
> I am joining Iyangura,
> Sister of Shemwindo.
> For Mukiti, my father, shall I go out of the way?
> You are powerless against Mwindo,
> Katitiiri and Mpumba
> And Rintea and Sheburenda![110]
> My father, I shall die [today], Mwindo!
> Aunt Iyangura howled, she said,
> Aunt Iyangura "of the body."[111]

Iyangura said: "If the sororal nephew of the Banamitandi is in this drum, let it arrive here so that I can see it before me." When the aunt cited the Banamitandi in this way, the drum refused to move in the

110. The current kinship term used by a woman for her brother's son or daughter is *mwána*, my child. Mwindo speaks about Mukiti as *titá*, my father; because Mukiti is his paternal aunt's husband, Mwindo pays respect to his aunt by using an honorific term for her husband. A paternal aunt's husband is normally identified with a maternal uncle. *Katitiiri . . .*: four symbolic personages, whose names (derived from insects) are specially selected by Mwindo to express his scorn for the pettiness of Mukiti's allies.

111. *Sínkárį Yangura wamúmubi/Aunt Iyangura "of the body"*: a double meaning lies in this expression. It indicates that Iyangura is a uterine sister of Mwindo's father; it is also a sign of tenderness.

direction of Iyangura. Inside the drum, Mwindo complained that this time his aunt missed (the mark). His aunt spoke again: "If you drum, (if) you are the sororal nephew of The-one-who-hears-secrets, come here; draw near me." When his aunt had mentioned in that way Those-who-hear-secrets, the drum still refused to draw near her. His aunt said anew: "If you really are the nephew of the Baniyana, come here before me." When Mwindo heard that, he went singing, in [his] leaving the pool:

I am going to my Aunt Iyangura,
Iyangura, sister of Shemwindo.
Kabarebare and Ntabare-mountain,
Where the husband of my senior sister sets *byoo*-traps.[112]
And a girl who is nice is a lady,
And a nice young man is a *kakoma*-pole.[113]
We are telling the story
That the Babuya have told [long ago].[114]
We are telling the story.
Kasengeri is dancing (wagging his) tail;
And you, see! (this) tail of *nderema*-fibers.[115]
Nkurongo-bird has gone to court *mususu*-bird;
Muhasha-bird has contracted asthma.[116]

112. *byoo-traps*: a trapping device currently in great use which is placed in the neighborhood of rivers and brooks. The names of mountains stand as designation for estates.

113. *marámi/lady*: Nyangaized French word *madame*. *kakoma-pole*: poles that form the framework of the house walls; they symbolize straightness. In these and many of the following verses, the narrator intersperses several reflections of his own in Mwindo's song. The narrator's joyful imagination is at work in these improvised passages.

114. *We are telling the story . . .*: *uano* is the term used for tales in general; the narrator says that what he is telling here is from (or part of [*múano*]) a story first told by people of the Babuya descent group, a group represented in the village where the narrator lived.

115. *Kasengeri*: the name of an animal sometimes used to designate a good dancer. *Is dancing (wagging his) tail*: the Nyanga expression *múconga* (on the tail, part of the tail) implies that when he dances, the most visible part is the tail. The narrator, who dances while singing this song, wears around the upper arm an armlet made of fibers cut from dried banana leaves. He praises himself as a good dancer and asks the onlookers to observe the movements of his arms adorned with the fiber armlets.

116. The narrator evokes certain tales about the *bulikoko*-bird, a symbol of good singing and of elegance, as opposed to *muhasha* who does not sing well (suffers from asthma, they say; gasps for breath all the time).

If I am at a loss for words in the great song,
If it dies out, may it not die out for me there.[117]
I cannot flirt with I-have-no-name;[118]
They are accustomed to speak to Mukiti (with) bells.
The tunes that we are singing,
The uninitiated-ones cannot know them.
I cannot be given *mburu*-monkey and still eat a lot,
I would remain satisfied with my flat belly.[119]
I have seen a rooster cock-a-doodle-dooing;
I also saw *muntori*-bird pointing him out.[120]
The little guardian of the rice (field)
Is never confused about
When sky has become day.
I see that meditations kill;
They killed the couple, otter and his mother.
If little pot travels too much,
It means little pot looks for a crack.[121]
He who (one day) ate *ntsuka*-fish does not sojourn long.
It is as though he had eaten the heart of the plunger.[122]
If Nyabunge coils (like) the whirlpools,
Then she loses her way home.
I learned that a catastrophe happened:
(One suffering from) frambesia and a leper on a bed.
If you hear the uproar of an argument,

117. *carwimbo/the great song*: omission of the high tone on *ca-* seems to mean that the song is personified. The various improvisations made here result from the fact that the narrator had lost the thread of Mwindo's song and of the story as a whole.

118. *ntsịra-rịna/I-have-no-name*: term with which women who have had many miscarriages are designated.

119. *Narịka nakéndéré bura/I would remain satisfied with my flat belly*: lit., I sat down, I was plaiting for the belly; "plait for the belly" is a stereotyped expression for "to admire." The meaning, then, of these two verses is that the narrator would like to be as perfect as the *mburu*-monkey, who is admired for his flat belly and is said to eat very little.

120. *birangira/cock-a-doodle-dooing*: an onomatopoeia. The two verses refer to a tale in which a rooster and a sparrow are the main actors.

121. References to three different tales.

122. A proverb; *ntsuka-fish* is a delicacy. If this fish is given to a guest, he will be sure to come to visit again.

It means the old woman has gotten more than the young
    mother.
I always sit down thinking about myself,
As (in the game) "throat and top."
I have cultivated bananas for the dragon
(So heavy) that a cluster had no one to carry it.
The *muhangu*-animal that tries to make the first banana
    fruits drop.
If the mother of the girl dies because of the young man,
It means an *atumbu*-insect falls from the *ntongi*-tree.[123]

When Mwindo was still in the act of going down [with] the river, the
moment he joined his aunt he went to arrive before her where she was.
His aunt seized the drum; her people gave her a knife; she slashed the
drum; removing the hide, she saw the multiple rays of the rising sun
and the moon. That is the beauty of the child Mwindo. Mwindo got
out of the drum, still holding his *conga*-scepter and his axe, together
with his little bag in which the rope was. When Kahungu saw Mwindo
meeting with his aunt, he went to bring the news to the *mutambo*-
elder who had been given to Iyangura to keep watch over her continually.[124] He arrived there, he gave him the news: "You, you (who) are
here, it is not (merely) a little man who appears over there; he is with
many stories and feats; you are dead." Hearing this news, Kasiyembe
said: "[You] envoy, you go! When you will have arrived at Mwindo's,
tell him he should not even try to pass this side; (otherwise) I shall tear
out his spinal column; I here am setting up traps, pits and pointed
sticks and razors in the ground, so that I shall know where he will
step." Seeing that, Katee went to appear where Mwindo was (and) told

123. Neither coherence nor consistency should be sought in this song. Three things
are brought out: the narrator has somewhat lost the thread of his story; he is hungry;
enjoying himself, he digresses by throwing out to his audience a number of personal
praises, personal reflections, collections of tales and proverbs. Nyanga songs are very
often nothing more than a loose piecing-together of totally unrelated verses. What
counts here is the singing, the dancing, the rhythm, and the music, not the verbaliza-
tions; the aim is not to convey ideas, but to enjoy sound and rhythm.

124. *kéntsé/the rising sun*: as a star the sun is known as *mwïshí*, a term that also
designates the heat carried by the sun. *kéntsé*: the light, the radiance of the sun; it is also
a spirit and may be used as a girl's name.

him: "You, Mwindo, your mates are holding secret council against you; they are even preparing pit traps against you, and pointed sticks and razors.[125] I (am) Katee, don't you always see me on the ground, in the depth of the earth?" Mwindo answered him: "Yes, I always see you; it is on the ground that you live." After having given Mwindo the news of that danger there in order to warn him, Katee also told him: "I am going to have a road go by, so that it emerges from the place where you are, and I want to make it come out inside the house of your aunt, at the base of the house pole." Mwindo said "Yes" to him. Mukei began to dig in the ground, inside it. Mwindo told his aunt Iyangura: "You, Aunt, proceed ahead; you be already on your way home; I shall meet you there; and that Kasiyembe threatening me over there, I shall first meet up with him; if he really has force, I shall deal with him (today)." He also said to his aunt: "Tell him, the one who is threatening me there, that he should prepare himself." Master Spider also emerged from within the pits, (he was) building bridges; he made them come out above the pits; the pits became merely bridges; he said to himself that it was there that Mwindo was going to play. "As far as I, Master Spider, am concerned, Mwindo cannot completely perish, since we are there." After his aunt had thus been told by Mwindo to proceed going, she did not tergiversate; she went home. Back there where Mwindo had remained, he took the road (made by) Katee; he came out in the house of his aunt, at Iyangura's, thanks to his *kahombo*.[126] When Kasiyembe saw him, he said: "Mwindo is already over here; now, from where has he emerged?" The people of his village said that they did not know from where he had emerged.

When Iyangura saw that her son Mwindo had already arrived, she said to him: "My son, don't eat food yet; come first to this side, so that we may dance (to the rhythm of) the drum. After Mwindo had heard

125. *mishíngá/stories and feats*: lit., a story in which the marvelous element and extraordinary deeds are underscored. *Kahungu*, the hawk, and *Katee*, the hedgehog, act here as messengers, in favor of Mukiti's allies and of Mwindo, respectively.

126. *muhéngéré/road*: a well-cleared trail, *ndákị/road*: a word derived from Lingala and generally used to designate a road built by Europeans. *utúnge/as far as I . . . am concerned*: a verbal form that means as much as, insofar as, equal to, as far as it concerns, in person. The Spider intends to say: as long as I am a spider, if I am truly a spider, in my capacity of being a spider, *kahombo*: the name of a tutelary spirit; the word is used here in the abstract to designate good fortune.

the words of his aunt, he left the house (and) appeared where his aunt was outdoors; he told his aunt that there he was, that he was going to dance without having eaten food, that he was going to faint with this drum.[127] His aunt replied to him: "Not at all! Dance all the same, [you] my son; and as for me, what shall I do then, since the one whom I was given to take care of me is saying that you must dance? What then shall we do? Dance all the same!" Hearing the word of his aunt, Mwindo said: "Oh! Right you are; let me first dance; hunger never kills a man." Mwindo sang; he howled, he said:

> Kasiyembe, you are powerless against Mwindo,
> For Mwindo is the Little-one-just-born-he-walked.
> Kasiyembe said: "Let us dance together."
> Shirungu, give us a morceau!
> If we die, we will die for you.
> Kasengeri is dancing with his *conga*-scepter,
> *Conga*-scepter of *nderema*-fibers.[128]
> I am saying farewell to Mpumba,
> My Mpumba with many raphia bunches.

Mwindo went round about in the middle of the pits; he marched (with the body) bent over the pits, without even being injured by the razors; he passed and passed everywhere where Kasiyembe had placed traps for him, without injuring himself. After Mwindo had passed and passed where traps had been set up for him, he danced; he agitated his *conga*-scepter to and fro, singing:

> It is Katee who is crackling of dried leaves,
> And it is Kantori who is Shebireo.[129]

127. The invitation for him to dance made by his aunt should not be considered as perfidy on her part. She knows that Kasiyembe has set traps for Mwindo and she wants Mwindo to give proof of his invulnerability. *That he was going to faint*: it is rare for Mwindo not to praise himself. Here, he is still boasting: he knows in advance that he will be saved and merely wants to give an impression of great drama.

128. This song is again a mixture of Mwindo's and the narrator's words. Mwindo provokes Kasiyembe. The narrator addresses himself to one of the percussionists, Shirungu; he stresses the difficulty of his task, but promises to accomplish it to please his audience.

129. The first verse is in praise of Katee, the hedgehog, who helped him and whose habit it is to draw dried leaves into its burrow. The second verse recalls a tale about the sparrow Kantori.

He also pointed out the Banamitandi, saying:

> You have seen that I am a follower of the Banamitandi.
> May Kahungu go to see now.
> May I see over there Shemumbo's village.[130]
> I am seeing that (among) the chimpanzees of the *ficus*-tree,
> The one who is repleted comes down.[131]

Iyangura told her son to eat some food, saying that since the time he arrived he had not spit his saliva while eating food.[132] Iyangura gave her son a bovine as a token of hospitality; he/she felled it. Eating it were those who were on the side, the maidens, who ate from it (for several days); he did not put [from] it in the mouth trying to eat from it. After Mwindo had eaten the hospitality gift of the bovine, which his aunt had offered to him, together with the maidens, Kasiyembe, the man of hatred, persisted in trying to kill him, saying:[133] "Is this the boy against whom I shall be impotent, whereas I heard that he came from the inside of a drum?"[134] Kasiyembe implored Nkuba, the lightning-hurler, saying: "You, Nkuba, you will have to come down; may you cut Mwindo into two pieces, in the house here where he is together with all these maidens who are with him here." When Mwindo heard the way in which Kasiyembe threatened him, over and over again, he told the maidens sitting with him in the house to sit down on one side with him because Kasiyembe wanted to bring lightning down on him. Then Mwindo said

---

130. *naréshiá/I am a follower*: i.e., someone who gives service and allegiance, receiving protection in return. *Shemumbo's village*: Shemumbo is the father (or giver) of a chief's ritual wife whose son is successor to the throne. The words have a double meaning: Mwindo refers to his father's village as the place of origin of his aunt Iyangura, who is now Mukiti's ritual wife; he also sees himself as the prospective chief of the land and looks upon his father merely as the provider of a ritual wife.

131. Reflection made by the narrator in reference to a tale.

132. *itúra oté/spit his saliva*: i.e., has not rinsed his mouth with water before eating.

133. It is to be understood that Mwindo does not eat the food. He receives the hospitality gift, but gives permission to the maidens to consume it. *After Mwindo had eaten the hospitality gift*: not to be understood literally; the verb *irisa/to eat* often means nothing more than to receive. *hima nóbikumí/together with the maidens*: there is some ambiguity here as to whether he and the maidens received the gift (the interpretation we prefer) or whether the gift he received from his aunt consisted of a cow and a group of maidens.

134. *muyú/the boy*: used in a pejorative sense; a male who is not yet an adult.

threateningly to Master Nkuba: "You, Nkuba, since you come down, you must come down on one side of the house; don't come down on the side where Mwindo is." Master Nkuba, on hearing the voice of Kasi-yembe, descended onto the house where Mwindo was; Mwindo pointed him out, saying: "You too will die the same (death); you are climbing on a hard tree." Master Nkuba came down seven times; each time he descended onto one side of the house in which Mwindo was, he did not come close to the place where he was; the fire burned on one side; that side became merely ashes. Where Iyangura, aunt of Mwindo, was sit-ting, tears rolled from her eyes and reached her legs, she saying that lo! her son was dying and that she had not even seen him well. Mwindo then came out of the house together with the maidens; he presented himself (before) the crowd of people; he declared about himself that there he was, the Little-one-just-born-he-walked. He said to his aunt to come close to where he was so that he could speak to her; his aunt came close to him; Mwindo spoke to her: "No more crying; it is you, my aunt, who are the reason Kasiyembe made this evil test come over me; in the day of tomorrow, if you will see me no more, it means that I am not worthy of Mwindo."[135] He told his aunt that within the twinkling of an eye, the mop of hair of Kasiyembe would already be burning.[136] Where Kasiyembe was, (people) were all of a sudden struck (by the fact that) in the mop of hair of Kasiyembe the fire was already flaring up; the tongues (of flame) rose into the air; all the lice and all the vermin that were nes-tled on his head, all were entirely consumed. When they saw the mop of hair of Kasiyembe burning, the people of Kasiyembe thought about fetching water in the jars in order to extinguish the fire on the head of Kasiyembe. When they arrived at the jars, in arriving there, there was no water left; all (the water) had dried up in the jars, there was not a drop (of water) left in them. They went straight to the herbaceous stalks of the plantains; they arrived there when they were (already) dried up, without a drop (of water) in them. They said: "What then! Spit some saliva on

135. *Nkúbá* is the divinity of lightning who is always described as being in a destruc-tive mood, ready to put his powers of devastation at the disposal of any solicitor, good or evil. Nkúbá tries to aid several enemies of Mwindo, but is always unsuccessful; later, he will become a friend and ally of Mwindo. *mirábyo/the lightning-hurler*: lit., efflores-cence of plants or flames of lightning.

136. Kasiyembe is described as a kind of fool, as an evil element (symbolized by the thick mop of hair).

(his) head!" Saliva was lacking among all the people; their mouths were wanting of saliva.[137] When they experienced this, they said: "This Kasi-yembe is about to die. Go and look for help for him at his Master's; it is at Mukiti's that there is a pool." They went there. Arriving there, they found Mukiti with butterflies and flies flitting about him; for him, too, the water had dried up; the whole pool had dried up, without even a drop (in it). When his aunt saw that, she went to beg before her son: "Widen your heart, you my son 'of the body,' you only child. By any chance did you come here where I am in order to attack us? Set your heart down; undo my husband together with his *mutambo*-elder, this one Kasiyembe; heal them without harboring further resentment against them."[138] After the aunt had finished humbly imploring her son, Mwindo had his heart go down; he woke up Kasiyembe, waving his *conga*-scepter above him; he sang:

> He who went to sleep wakes up.
> You are impotent against Mwindo,
> Mwindo is the Little-one-just-born-he-walked.

"Wake up thanks to my *conga* here of *nderema*-fibers."

> He who went to sleep wakes up.
> Look, I am playing with (my) *conga*-scepter.

Suddenly, Kasiyembe was saved. And the jars, water returned again in them; and the herbaceous stalks of all the plantains, in them again was water; and there where Mukiti was, the water came back again for him; the river was full again. When they saw that feat, they were much astonished, saying: "Lo! Mwindo, he too, is a great man."[139] Kasiyembe

---

137. The richness of verbal expression is well illustrated in this short passage. To say that jars, banana trees, and mouths were lacking liquid, the narrator uses four verbal phrases: not to remain (*nti kúsįrá*), not in them (*angá . . . Mubyó*), to fail (to catch animals) (*ihína*), and to miss (*irúka*).

138. *kokórá émutima/widen your heart*: lit., unknot, stretch your heart; has the same meaning as *sįcá émutima/set your heart down*. In Nyanga thinking the heart "is knotted" or "is high" when one is angry or in deep emotional shock.

139. *wábǔme/a great man*: i.e., a full-fledged adult male, and not a boy as Kasiyembe called him. The song is a recurrent magic formula, that Mwindo uses to regenerate his enemies. The narrator, who is adorned with fiber armlets and is dancing with a *conga*-scepter (like the one the hero Mwindo is supposed to have), again identifies himself and his own dancing with Mwindo's actions.

gave Mwindo a salute, saying: "Hail! hail! oh! Mwindo." And Mwindo answered, "Yes." After he had accomplished that deed, Mwindo said to his aunt that tomorrow he would be going to Tubondo to fight with his father, because his father had thrown him away twice; now he would in his turn go to stand up against him. The aunt told him: "Oh! my father, you will be impotent at your father's, in Tubondo; you, (just) yesterday's child, born just a while ago, is it you who will be capable of Tubondo, village with seven meeting places?[140] Iyangura! I had you taken out from within the drum; as far as I am concerned, I say 'No,' strongly; never again try to go alone; the lonely path is never nice." When Mwindo heard the way in which his aunt was speaking, he refused; he wiped out his aunt('s words) (by) humming to himself. The aunt told him: "You, (my) young man, to give birth to a son is to rest. Do not go to fight with your father; if you go, at any rate, then I also shall go with you to see how your father will be cutting you into pieces." She went to tell the maidens to pack up her household objects, so as to go with Mwindo, because the lonely path is not nice; it never fails to find something that could kill a man. When the sky had become daylight, they had breakfast before the journey of returning back to Tubondo. Mwindo went together with his aunt, together with his servants who were chanting the refrain. Mwindo sang:

> *Ntiriri-liana* has become *mubanga*-rope,
> And *musara*-liana has become a *mukendo*-bag.[141]
> Scribe, march!
> I am going over there to Tubondo;
> I shall fight over there in Tubondo,
> Even though Tubondo has seven entries.
> We are saying, oh Bira!
> Aunt, give me advice

140. *karamo karamŏ ka/hail! hail*: this is the current Nyanga greeting; *karamo* means health, salvation, life (good and long); *aé/yes* is the current answer after the greeting of *karamo. é titá/oh! my father*: father, mother, and paternal aunt currently call their own son or nephew "father" when they want to please him or to give him advice, *ubútwăyo tété-tétéyo/born just a while ago*: rare usage of *tététété* normally meaning "fast."

141. *mushúkĭra/young man*: stress is on "growing"; currently used to designate an adolescent. *ntiriri-liana has become . . ., mucara-liana has become . . .*: these two lianas are not normally used to fabricate a carrying rope or a shoulder bag; Mwindo intends to say that the order and balance of events and actions are upset.

To fight with the people downstream;
They carry spears and shields.
In Ihimbi where dwelt Birori,
I shall die (today), Mushumo.
On Ntsuri-hill where dwelt Ruronga,
(In) Munongo where dwelt Shecara,
Bitumbi-hill of Shemene Ndura,
And the old ones fight because of a wind.
On Mbare-hill where dwelt Karai,
He was the one who gives much tribute of words.
Mbare-hill is together with Irimwe-hill, his kinsman,
Tunkundu-hill is together with Nteko-hill, his kinsman.
May I mention Mabura Banyore,
Homeland of my mothers,
Kabotyo Munyangoro
Nyabuke Kamwikoti.[142]
Big legs ravaged Mpurwa,
And the baboon ruined Kamuri.[143]
Sky became day, I was (still) speaking
Like the sound (of) Mukuki.[144]
The sky in this village takes a long time to become day:
It is the single man who is cooking hard-to-cook food.[145]
Mikere-river is together with Mboru-river, his kinsman,
And Batoi-river is together with Tua-river, his kinsman.
Who will take me to Bukuca, to Ngara?
Mbuhi is of both Mutatea and Mwindo,

142. The narrator again inserts personal recollections in Mwindo's song. He speaks about Ihimbi, the area from where he comes, and about the characters whom he met there or whose fame was well established, e.g., Birari, the diviner, and Karai, the daredevil. In the names mentioned here there are many *quid pro quo*'s, e.g., Kabotyo Munyangoro, Nyabuke Kamwikoti: we consider these to be the double names of two individuals, a male and a female; in fact, a valid interpretation could also be the following: Kabotyo of the Nyangoro group, she who is famed (*nya-*) for the beads around the neck. *shé-mutúro wábinwa/who gives much tribute of words*: this is not to praise, nor is it to criticize the individual who speaks too much, but refers to one who gives tribute in words, one who is helpful because of his skill as judge and speaker.

143. *Cámwindí/big legs*: praise name for an elephant. Mpurwa and Kamuri are names of estates.

144. *Mukuki*: one of the Nyanga closed associations.

145. This is a frequently heard proverb that evokes the sad fate of the single man.

Kirambo is of Mamboreo.[146]
May the people of Ntande not regret (the lack of) meat,
(For) they have had a woman who fishes (with a net).
Mpinga (is) land
Whereas Nkasa is the natal village of Burongo
And of Mwindo.
May the Batembo not regret (the lack of) meat.
They hold Mutumba and Kunju.[147]
And Birere-hill of Rukobakoba;
I cannot fish with the Baroba.
From Europe there come (all kinds of things)!
The sun is setting downstream
From the Batika-Rukari.
Maere, little girl of Rukunja,
Maere, what did you eat when you came?
I have not eaten anything extraordinary;
I have eaten a goat for sharing purposes,
And I also ate *mususa*-vegetables (picked in) the village.
They were full of sand and slime.
To a trap that is not well set
Katiti-pigeon (only) leaves its tail.
The *nkurongo*-birds of this village are mean;
The *nkurongo*-birds, as soon as they have seen people,
Flutter (their) tails.
In Kumbukumbu of the Batobo
Where dwelt Nkuru and Rukari.[148]

146. The narrator refers to certain rivers that are the limits of the landed estates con-
trolled by descent groups to which he is personally linked. In mentioning the mountain
Mbuhi, he designates one of the limits between the Nyanga and the Funa (a subgroup of
the Hunde tribe); part of this mountain is in Nyanga control, part belongs to the Funa.

147. *a woman who fishes (with a net)*: women normally fish with baskets and participate in communal fishing with poison, *buróngo/land*: Nyangaized Swahili word for soil,
land. In two consecutive verses the word is used both as the generic term for land and as
the name of a person. *Batembo*: one of the descent groups found in Nyanga country.

148. *Burdÿa/Europe*: Nyangaized Swahili word, *mpéné kishángįre/a goat for sharing
purposes*: i.e., a goat or other animal that is not the object of taboos or prescriptions
concerning who can eat from it and under what circumstances it can be eaten (chickens
are never in the category of *kishángįre* because there are strict prescriptions for in-laws
concerning their distribution). The narrator is complaining that he did not get a special
hospitality gift, i.e., that he was compelled to eat with the others. *mususa-vegetables*: a
vegetable that is a major ingredient for Nyanga dishes. Some are grown behind the

Mwindo sang:

> Scribe, march!
> I am going with the aunt.
> The Little-one has slept all prepared for the journey.
> Oh! my father, the Little-one set out right after awakening.
> (I warn you) we are already underway, we,
> To Bat of the Baniyana.[149]

During this journey that Mwindo was making in spite of all with his aunt, evening went to find him at his maternal uncles, the Baniyana. He slept there after they had killed a goat of hospitality for him. After he, together with his paternal aunt and the servants of the aunt, had eaten that goat, Mwindo said to his maternal uncles: "I am going to fight Shemwindo in Tubondo; forge me, you [who are] blacksmiths of large light spears, you my uncles.[150] The Baniyana said that they were going to forge him. They dressed him in shoes made entirely of iron and pants of iron; they also forged him an iron shirt and a hat of iron. They told him: "Since you are going to fight your father, may the spears that they will unceasingly hurl at you go striking on this iron (covering) that is on (your) body." After the uncles had finished forging him, they said that they could remain no more; they would be going with him so that they might see the way in which they would knead him. In the morning, Mwindo began the journey together with

---

houses, like the one referred to here; others are grown in the banana groves. The latter are much more appreciated; the former are used only when one is in a hurry or short of supplies. The narrator complains again about the kind of food he has received. As noted, most of the verses of this song have nothing to do with the story, but are merely the narrator's personal reflections about people, landed estates, stories. He also expresses his frustration at the lack of consideration with which he is being treated.

149. *twará twendánge băte (I warn you) we are already underway, we*: lit., we are eating we are going; the expression *twará* and the verb to go are often used to say that one is already on his way, that one is going without further delay. The image conveyed here is that whereas people normally sit down quietly to eat, at this point there is no question of sitting; one is moving and can only hurriedly take a bit of food from a friend or relative while passing through the village.

150. *forge me*: the hero asks that his maternal uncles *forge him*, i.e., make him strong and resistant. The image of the hero being forged occurs in other tales. The bats are always represented as blacksmiths because, as the Nyanga say, of the kinds of sounds and excrements they produce.

his uncles and his aunt Iyangura, and the servants of his aunt. Mwindo went singing; he howled, he said:

> I shall fight over there at Shemwindo's.
> The cattle that Shemwindo possesses,
> May they join Mwindo.
> Oh! scribe, march!

When they were on the point of arriving there, when they already had the village in sight, Mwindo's aunt said to Mwindo: "Oh! my father, let's get out of here, look how there is dizziness over there in your father's village; Tubondo over there is a village of seven ways out; there are many people over there; they will destroy us." Mwindo answered his aunt: "I, Mwindo, I never am afraid of a big child with whom I have not yet fought; I want to try this Shemwindo out first; he is too much spoiled by pride."[151] Mwindo went on, singing:

> We are going over there to Tubondo
> Where dwelt Shemwindo.

When they arrived in the glen, he said: "Let us spend the night in this village." His aunt howled, she said: "Where will we sleep, here there is no house? Lo! Kiruka-nyambura has arrived, bearer of rain that never ceases."[152] The aunt shouted, she said: "Oh! my father, where shall we sleep? The rain has just rumbled, (the) young woman is destitute."[153] Mwindo looked around, he said that he wanted (to have) houses: (and) the houses built themselves. Mwindo said that his uncles (should take) that row there, and his aunt that other row; and Mwindo's house planted itself in the middle of them. His aunt shouted saying: "Yes, my father Mwindo, hail for (these) [our] houses. Lo!

151. *pantaró/pants; shįmįshį/shirt*: Nyangaized French words *pantalon* and *chemise*, respectively, *nkobįra/hat*: Nyangaized Kingwana word *kofia* (*kofera*, hat), *look how there is dizziness over there . . .*: the dizziness is felt by the onlookers when they are in the glen and look up the hill at the huts built on the steep crest.

152. *Where dwelt Shemwindo*: in his vision of things to happen, Mwindo sees his father's village already destroyed and his father fleeing. *Kiruka-nyambura*: lit., Kiruka, she who drags along rain; the Nyanga believe that rain is caused by an old woman who lives in the sky.

153. *munyeré/the young woman*: a word of the Hunde vocabulary (*munyére*): the high tone has been placed on the last syllable to enhance the ironic effect of her exclamation.

Shemwindo has brought forth a hero; Kahombo, my father, I shall give you (some) paste. Let us go with our prestigious man; may our prestigious man escape thunder and lightning![154] Shemwindo brought forth a hero who is never afraid, and Mwindo himself is a hero."[155] When they were there in the glen, the houses having built themselves, Mwindo's aunt said to him: "Oh! my father Mwindo, let us get away; you are powerless against this mass of people who are in Tubondo." Mwindo said that first he would try. Iyangura, Mwindo's aunt, said to him: "Oh! my father Mwindo, what shall we eat then? Look! the great number of your uncles here, and I too, Iyangura, have a line of people, and you, Mwindo, you have drummers and singers with you; what will this whole group eat?" Mwindo, hearing what his aunt had just told him, agreed, saying: "You are not lying, [you] my aunt; I see that the whole group that is with us is already hungry." He lifted his eyes to the sky; he said to himself that he first wanted to have all the food that was over there in Tubondo come; so (the food) having joined him, he would go to fight with them. Mwindo sang while transporting the food that was with his father. His aunt shouted, she said: "Oh! my father, what shall we eat (today)?" Mwindo howled, he sang:

> The pastes that are in Tubondo,
> May the pastes join Mwindo,
> Mwindo, the Little-one-just-born-he-walked.
> The animals that are in Tubondo,
> May the animals join Mwindo.

154. *mutangá/row*: technical term for a row of huts. *muraj/hero*: the term emphasizes the idea of strength and aggressiveness; e.g., bees may be called *baraj*; the soldiers introduced by the Europeans also went under that name. *Kahombo*: the name of the spirit of good fortune; Iyangura uses the term here to praise Mwindo as a benefactor. *I shall give you some paste*: when a young woman says this to her father, she means that she will bear children, her father's grandchildren on whose behalf he will eat banana paste during the ablution ceremonies. *karánĭ wĭtŭ/our prestigious man*: lit., our clerk; it is a Nyangaized Kingwana word. In the rural community the position of clerk (i.e., a man with some degree of education) had become synonymous with status and prestige.

155. *Shemwindo brought forth a hero ... and Mwindo himself is a hero*: a double meaning is contained in these words. On the one hand Iyangura praises both Shemwindo and Mwindo (she always manifests respect and a kind of awe for her brother, and is therefore torn between her love for Mwindo and her attachment to Shemwindo). On the other hand, Iyangura seems to state that Mwindo does not merely owe his herioc qualities to being the son of Shemwindo.

The meats that Shemwindo stores,
May the meats join Mwindo Mboru,
Mwindo, the Little-one-just-born-he-walked.
The wood that Shemwindo keeps,
Oh! father, may it join Mwindo Mboru,
For Mwindo is the Little-one-just-born-he-walked.
And the fire that Shemwindo possesses,
May the fire also join Mwindo.
And the water that Shemwindo possesses,
May the water also join Mwindo Mboru.
The jars that are at Shemwindo's
May the jars join Mwindo,
Mwindo, the Little-one-just-born-he-walked.
The clothes that are at Shemwindo's,
May the clothes join Mwindo,
Mwindo is going to fight!
The wooden dishes that are in Tubondo,
May the wooden dishes also join Mwindo,
Oh father! the Little-one-just-born-he-has-walked
Hopes to be victorious.
The beds that Shemwindo possesses,
May the beds join Mwindo.
And the wicker plates that Shemwindo possesses,
May the wicker plates also join Mwindo.
And the salt that Shemwindo possesses,
May the salt also join Mwindo,
The Little-one-just-born-he-walked.[156]

It was in this way that Mwindo was speaking!

And the chickens that Shemwindo possesses,
May the chickens also join Mwindo.
The cheerleaders are in unison;
They thus having achieved unison long ago.
The cheerleaders are in unison;
They have achieved harmony in the middle of the village.
That which-will-die and that which-will-be-saved,
May it join Iyangura here,

156. This song gives a short inventory of some of the most significant items in the diet and the technology of the Nyanga. The idea of ownership is rendered by the verbs *kuba na* (to be with) and *ibíka* (to keep, to guard, to have in trust, to stock, to lay down).

Iyangura, sister of Shemwindo.
The goats that are at Shemwindo's,
May the goats join Mwindo.
The cattle that are in Tubondo,
May the cattle join Mwindo.
The cattle bellowed, saying,
"Oh father! let us join Mwindo."
The dogs that are in Tubondo,
May the dogs join Mwindo.
The dogs barked, saying,
"Oh father! let us join Mwindo."
We are seated, stretching out our voices
Like the diggers of pits (for trapping).
The banana groves that are in Tubondo,
May the banana groves join Mwindo.
And the tobacco also that is at Shemwindo's,
May the tobacco also join Mwindo.
The *mukusa*-asp swallowed froth;
Anger is in the heart.
And the pipes that Shemwindo possesses,
May the pipes also join Mwindo.
The spears that are at Shemwindo's,
May the spears join Mwindo.
The adzes that are at Shemwindo's,
May the adzes join Mwindo.
The billhooks that are at Shemwindo's,
Oh father! may the billhooks join Mwindo;
May there be none left to go gardening.
The pruning knives that are at Shemwindo's,
May the pruning knives join Mwindo,
Little pruning knife, little scraper of *mbubi*-lianas.
May the little pruning knife join Mwindo.
The little dog bells that Shemwindo possesses,
May the little dog bells join Mwindo;
May there be nobody left to go hunting.
The bags that Shemwindo possesses,
May the bags also join Mwindo.
The razors that Shemwindo possesses,
May the razors also join Mwindo;
May there be nobody left who is shaved.
The *butea*-rings that Shemwindo possesses,

Oh father! the *butea*-rings,
May they be ready to join Mwindo;
May there be nobody left who wears (them).
The necklaces that Shemwindo possesses,
May the necklaces also join Mwindo;
May there be nobody left who wears (them).
The needles that Shemwindo possesses,
May the needles also join Mwindo;
May there be nobody left to do hook work.
The fire drill that Shemwindo possesses,
May the fire drill also join Mwindo;
May there be nobody left who makes fire.
The hoes that Shemwindo possesses,
Oh father! the hoes,
May they join Mwindo;
May there be nobody left who hoes.
The pots that Shemwindo possesses,
May the pots also join Mwindo;
May there be nobody left who cooks.
The baskets that Shemwindo possesses,
May the baskets join Mwindo;
May there be nobody left who goes to work.
The *mumanga*-piercer that Shemwindo possesses,
May the *mumanga*-piercers join Mwindo;
May there be nobody who bores shafts.
Let us recite from the story
That the Babuya are used to reciting.
The *bisara*-billhooks that Shemwindo possesses,
May the *bisara*-billhooks join Mwindo;
May there be nobody who prunes banana trees.
And the bellows that Shemwindo possesses,
May the bellows also join Mwindo;
May there be nobody left who smiths.
And the hammers that are at Shemwindo's,
May the hammers also join Mwindo;
May there be nobody who smiths.
And the blacksmiths whom Shemwindo has,
May the blacksmiths also join Mwindo;
May there be nobody who smiths.
The *nkendo*-knives that are in Tubondo,
The *nkendo*-knives that Shemwindo possesses,

May the *nkendo*-knives join Mwindo;
May there be nobody who plaits.
The raphia palm trees that are at Shemwindo's,
May the raphia palm trees join Mwindo;
May there be nobody who plaits
Or who traps.
And the drums that are in Tubondo,
Oh father! the drums,
May they join Mwindo;
May there be nobody who dances.[157]

Mwindo and his uncles and his aunt and the servants who had arrived with them, the singers and the drummers, when (the latter) opened their eyes—all the things that were in Tubondo at Shemwindo's (had) joined them there where they were. When the aunt of Mwindo saw all those things, she said to her son Mwindo: "Oh father! You will suffer because of those things (belonging to) other people which you are gathering together." Those who were with Mwindo in the vale were sick with the indisposition of being gorged with food; they were not cold any more; they refound (their) heat; they said: "Lo! Mwindo is a man who does not lie when he says that he is the Little-one-just-born-he-walked; he always has something to rely upon.[158] The one who will try to climb on him will be the first to die on the great road; he is not a man to provoke." When Mwindo had seen that the things of his father had come to join him, he said that his father (now) remained over there merely as a destitute person. He said to his aunt that he wanted his uncles to go ahead and fight first, and that he, Mwindo, would remain with his aunt for a while here in the vale so that he might first see the way in which his uncles handled their force. After he had thus sent his uncles out to go to fight, his uncles departed to fight, and he remained with his aunt in the vale. Where his uncles

157. This song continues the inventory of Nyanga material culture. In the beginning, the inventory is interrupted by the narrator's praise for the singers and percussionists who accompany him (*The cheerleaders are in unison . . .*). *We are seated*: another reflection by the narrator about the length of the story and his fear that it may become monotonous. *The mukusa-asp*: reference to a story.

158. *káríkíré kínyihíré/he always has something to rely upon*: lit., he is sitting he thinks about himself, i.e., he is sure of his force.

passed, they fought on land and in the air, but the people of Tubondo said: "You will not solve the case today."[159]

After a while, Mwindo's uncles were completely wiped out; they died; the people of Tubondo wiped them out. One of Mwindo's uncles escaped in the middle of the war, being already seriously injured; he fled to Mwindo to report the news to him. He arrived there and said: "There where we have gone, the people of Tubondo have overcome us, all the people—your uncles—are dried up." When Mwindo's aunt saw this messenger—the blood had covered his whole body—and also heard the news of how the people had completely dried up, she exclaimed: "Oh, father Mwindo, I have told you that when I said that you are helpless against the people of Shemwindo over there; you said, 'Not at all'; first pick up this *nkebe*-tooth here, this first achievement; look how they have been wiped out."[160] Mwindo said to his aunt: "I too, I shall go to find out first the reason why my uncles are all wiped out, and if Shemwindo does not come up face to face with me, then I am not Mwindo." His aunt said to him: "Oh, father Mwindo, don't! You will be the reason for which the whole group that has arrived with us (will) be wiped out. If you vex the people over there in Tubondo, then we are all on the verge of dying." Mwindo did not listen to the mouth of his aunt; he said that he was going to fight: "You, aunt, remain with my axe here and my little bag in which there is a rope; and I, Mwindo, am leaving with my *conga* here." Mwindo went. Where he headed, he went to climb up to Tubondo. As soon as the people of that village saw Mwindo arriving at the village entrance, they pointed him out; they said to Shemwindo: "See that little man alone there who makes his appearance at the village entrance through which the war came." Shemwindo answered his people: "What will a little man do all by

159. *to die on the great road*: i.e., to die in solitude and abandonment. *kihuhúru/a destitute person*: lit., a man heavily intoxicated with beer. *bútíngengá . . . bátínge/the way in which his uncles handled*: interesting syntactic construction found *passim* in the epic; translated, the duplication of the verb with different prefixes and markers means: how they take/handle (it) . . . when they take/handle (it), *ékwantsí někwiyo/on land and in the air*: everywhere; it is not to be understood as if the uncles were flying, *mutûkeri ro/you will not solve the case*: lit., you will not cut it; *ro* bears on the word *ubántsá*, case, palaver.

160. *mubándá/seriously injured*: used for an injured animal as well as for a human being. *bákusįka/are dried up*: *isįka* is said of water that is absorbed into the soil, *nkebe-tooth*: i.e., the first fruits of your efforts; this is said ironically.

himself? Even if he comes, we shall cut his throat so that he will die." His people answered him: "There from where *bisibisi*-insects emerge, one day red ants will issue; this one little man can make us run in this village without our being able to do anything against him." Shemwindo answered his people: "Let this little fool go swaggering toward the garbage heap." Mwindo emerged at the village entrance while singing; he agitated his *conga* round about. When Mwindo arrived in Tubondo, he got into the middle of the village; he said to the people of that village that he wanted to dance (to the rhythm of) a drum. The people of that village answered him: "You are helpless against our drums here, you (are a) little fool." Mwindo answered them that this was an insult, that he had not even had time to rest.[161] The people of that village told him that there was no drum there. To that Mwindo said that the drums would be coming. Mwindo went on speaking in that way with the people of that village, his father being in his compound. Mwindo sang:

> He is climbing up here in Tubondo,
> He is going to fight with Shemwindo.

While he was singing, he went on enunciating (distinctly): "May what will die and what will be saved join Iyangura." He raised his voice to the sky, he sang:

> What will never die but will be saved,
> May it, oh father, join Iyangura,
> Iyangura, sister of Shemwindo,
> Mother mine of the cradling string.[162]
> Oh! father, what will die and will be saved,
> May it join its aunt,
> Sister of Shemwindo!
> My junior and my senior sisters,
> Be ready to join me.
> What will never die but will be saved,
> May it join Iyangura,

---

161. *he had not even had time to rest*: Mwindo expresses his surprise that they are so fast in challenging and slandering him.

162. *nyámwako/mother . . . of the cradling-string*: this is the highest honorific name a person can give to his mother or aunt. Nyanga women carry their babies tied on their backs in a network of flat-woven raphia bands; these bands have an exceptional religious and emotional value and are said to be part of the child's personality.

Aunt, sister of Shemwindo.
My senior brother, come,
What will die and will be saved,
May it join Aunt Iyangura.
May you, oh my mothers, come!
What will not die but be saved,
May it join Aunt Iyangura.
I die, oh Bira!
What has been said will be said again.
Let me fight here in Tubondo,
Even if Tubondo has seven entrances.
The counselors have hesitated (to counsel) Shemwindo.
What will die and be saved,
May it join Aunt Iyangura.
The counselors retreated (before) Shemwindo.
What will die and be saved,
May it join Aunt Iyangura.
Nkuba, my friend, may you be victorious.[163]
Hatred is in the heart.
When I shall have a bridge built for myself,
He who crosses it will cut himself.
I implored Aunt Iyangura,
Aunt Iyangura, may you be blessed.[164]

Mwindo shouted, saying:

Hatred is in the heart.
My friend, Nkuba, may you be victorious.
I shall fight here in Tubondo,
Even if Tubondo has seven entrances.
Here in Tubondo seven lightning flashes!
I shall fight here in Tubondo.
I want seven lightning flashes right now!
Mwindo reviewed (the causes of) his griefs;

163. *Botó ná bababá bâní/My junior and my senior sisters: motó*, junior, can bear both on male or female siblings or parallel cousins; *babá* can bear only on senior female siblings or parallel cousins. We know that Mwindo had several sisters, all born before him of different wives of his father; it is implied that he also had junior brothers, *ubúráne* is a verb that has bearing on a secular trial in which no spirits are involved; it means to win a trial, to be acquitted.

164. *ukasananga/may you be blessed: ikasana* means to win the favor of the spirits.

The counselors retreated (before) Shemwindo.
The counselors did not know how to counsel.
It's you who will turn into dried leaves,
—In the river—
My father threw me into the drum.
I shall fight here in Tubondo;
May Tubondo turn into dried leaves,
Merely.
The counselors retreated (before) Shemwindo;
The counselors did not know how to counsel;
May the counselors turn into dried leaves.
My friend, Nkuba, may you be victorious.
Hatred is in the heart.
I implored Aunt Iyangura,
What will die and be saved,
May it join Iyangura,
Aunt, sister of Shemwindo.
My little fiery father,
My little father threw me into the grave.
My father believed that I would die;
My little father threw me into the grave.
My little father believed that I would die.
If you believe that girls are (worthy) beings
It is (because) oh father, they bring in goods.[165]

In his heart he was saying that girls were people worthier than he, that
they transcended him; "You will find out (about it) today."

Girls are (worthy) beings
Oh, father, it is (because) they bring in goods.[166]
Tubondo, seven lightning flashes!

Mwindo raised his eyes into heaven (and) said:

My friend, Nkuba,
Here in Tubondo seven lightning flashes!

165. In this song, Mwindo predicts the coming destruction of his father's village; he
asks for the help of the spirit of lightning and summarizes his grievances against his
father and his father's counselors. He states that his father, because of his greed, had only
wanted daughters, since they are the providers of marriage payments.

166. *bákéngí behe/they bring in goods: ịké* means to rain; *ịké behe* is a stereotyped
expression to designate the process of providing and receiving marriage payments.

While Mwindo was looking up into the sky, he (also) stretched his *conga* toward there. From the sky at Nkuba's, things came; there appeared seven lightning flashes; they descended on Tubondo in the village. Tubondo turned into dust, and the dust rose up; all who lived there turned into mere dust. Where Shemwindo was sitting in (his) compound, he exclaimed: "There is no time for lingering here." Having spoken like that, he went down behind the house; he went without looking back. Where he fled, he went to arrive where there was a *kikoka*-plant. He tore it out; he entered at its root's base. After he had become victorious in Tubondo, Mwindo praised himself in the middle of the village; he said: "This time the one who climbs on me, the one who digs into me while fighting with me, will be wearing himself out in vain." He spoke like this when the corpses of his uncles who were the first to die had already begun to decay. Mwindo went down to where his aunt had remained in the glen in order that they would rise up to the peak. He arrived at his aunt's; the aunt asked him: "Good news there from where you are coming?"[167] Mwindo answered her that Tubondo was on fire. He also told them: "Now let's go up to Tubondo which is high up; let's get away from here in the glen."[168] When the aunt began preparing her belongings, Mwindo forbade her; he said to her: "Leave the things; they themselves will join us over there in Tubondo." Having spoken like that, he went, and his aunt followed him together with the group of servants who had come with them. They climbed up to Tubondo; they arrived there. When they were already in Tubondo, the things that they had left in the glen joined them. Mwindo said that he could not chase his father so long as he had not resuscitated his uncles. He woke them up beating them (with his) *conga* and singing:

> He who went to sleep awakes,
> My uncle, my mother, wake up.
> I have been testing the Baniyana.

167. *kikoka-plant*: a kind of fern that grows in the forest and is found in the clearing around the villages. The Nyanga use the plant for brewing beer and in various magical contexts. In tales, heroes and other characters are said to hide in this plant or, more often, to go underground by entering it. *mahyó/good news*: a Hunde word for greeting.

168. *kwákangámá/which is high up*: *ịkangama*, to be taller, in a comparison between two people.

> My uncle, my mother, forge me![169]
> Shemwindo, you are powerless against Mwindo,
> Mwindo is the Little-one-just-born-he-walked.
> My uncle, my mother, forge me.
> You are a blacksmith of light spears.

Mwindo finished waking up all his maternal uncles; they resuscitated. Where Shemwindo had fled, he went harming himself running into everything; he went to arrive at Musia's, the place where no one ever clusters around the fire.[170] In Tubondo, where Mwindo settled with his aunt, with his uncles, and with his servants, singers, and drummers, he told them: "Let's join Shemwindo whither he headed to Muisa's; let us go in search of him." His aunt handed over to him his bag in which there was the rope; she also handed over to him his axe, whereas he still clasped his *conga*, he its owner. Mwindo said to his aunt: "You, my aunt, remain here in this village in Tubondo with these uncles here and the group of singers and drummers, along with whom we came; because you are used to eating terrestrial foods, you are not capable of all the adventures and the dangers that I am used to experiencing wherever I pass."[171] Mwindo said to his aunt: "You, my aunt, you stay here in the village of your birth, in Tubondo; here is the rope; remain with one end, holding it in your hand, whereas I shall follow my father where he fled to Muisa's; if (one day) you feel that this rope has become still, if it does not move anymore, then pay no more attention to where I have gone; lo! the fire has dwindled; I am dead then." After he had spoken like that,

169. *nashiángá/I have been testing*: this seems a logical interpretation, since his maternal uncles had earlier challenged Mwindo saying that they would accompany him to see him beaten by Shemwindo. The verb used here is either *ishia*, to test, to put to proof, or *ishía*, to give allegiance to a chief or other person. The latter interpretation also makes sense, since Mwindo is a sororal nephew of the Baniyana and can consider himself to be their subject.

170. *nti íyé wícábíránge/harming himself running into everything*: *ícába* literally means to cut (firewood); the reflexive form of the verb is often used to describe the way in which an injured animal bumps against bushes and trees. *Muisa*: one of the Nyanga divinities, who is said to live in a cold, desolate, subterranean place where fire is unknown.

171. Before engaging in his subterranean peregrinations. Mwindo is compelled to leave his aunt and all his other companions behind, because they do not have his supernatural gifts ("they eat terrestial foods"). He does, however, remain in contact with his aunt by means of a rope, *ébiburá/dangers*: lit., the fire sparks of the blacksmith's forge; the blacksmith is said to be immune to them.

Master Sparrow alit where he was, he told him: "Come here for me to show you the path that your father took and where he entered at the base of the root of the *kikoka*- plant; indeed, when your father fled, I, Sparrow, was on top of the roof; your father fled while I was seeing him stumbling." After Sparrow had given him the news, Mwindo in [his] leaving said farewell to his aunt; he held one end of the rope and the aunt remained holding (the other) end of the rope. Mwindo rushed hurriedly toward the village exit. When he arrived at the *kikoka*-plant, where his father had entered, he too pulled out the *kikoka*-plant; he entered at its base; he passed through; he went to appear at the well. Arriving there, he met Kahindo, daughter of Muisa.[172] Kahindo embraced him, saying: "This is my welcome, Mwindo." Mwindo in reply said "Yes." Kahindo was sick with yaws; the yaws started at her tooth and went up to the perineum; they descended the legs (and) went up to the toes of the sole of the feet.[173] When Mwindo tried to go through, Kahindo forbade, saying, "No, no." She said to him: "Where are you going?" Mwindo answered her that he was going to Muisa's to look for his father because it was here in this village of Muisa that he was. She told him again: "Stop first here where I am. Over there in Muisa's village one never goes through; is it you who will (succeed) in getting through there like that, with all (your) pride?" Kahindo said to Mwindo: "Now you are going to Muisa's. When you will have arrived there, having entered the meeting place, if you see a very big man and tall too, curled up in the ashes near the hearth, it is he who is Muisa; and if he greets you, if he says: 'Blessing (be) with you, my father,' you too will answer, 'Yes, my father'; and when he will have left you a stool, then you will refuse it; you will tell him: 'No, my father; will the head of a man's father become a stool?' When he will have handed over to you a little gourd of banana beer for you to drink, you will refuse, answering: 'No, my father, even though a person is one's child, is that a reason why he should drink the

---

172. *Kahindo*: the Hunde name for Kahombo, the female spirit of good fortune among the Nyanga. Both are also personal names given to males as well as to females who stand in a particular ritual relationship to this spirit.

173. *wámukókére/embraced him*: this form of greeting is normal between mother and child, but not, as here, between persons who are strangers to each other, *karíbŭ nko/ this is my welcome: karibu* is a Swahili term for "come in." *binyóra/yaws*: children usually have them now; the disease is more rare in adults. To criticize somebody because of ingratitude, the Nyanga say: "I cured your yaws."

urine of his father?' After Muisa will have recognized you in that way, he will say to you: 'Blessing, blessing, Mwindo'; and you will answer him: 'And to you blessing, blessing also, father.' When he will have given you paste to eat, you will answer him: 'Even though a person is one's child, is that a reason why he should eat the excrements of his father?'"[174]

After Mwindo had heard Kahindo speaking these useful words to him, he said to himself that he could not leave without washing the yaws of Kahindo. Mwindo began washing the yaws of Kahindo; he smoothed them, taking away all the scabs of the yaws. After Mwindo had washed the yaws of Kahindo in that way, after he had also healed them entirely, Mwindo passed ahead of her; he went and climbed up to Muisa's; he arrived there and headed for the meeting place. Muisa, seeing him, greeted him with "Blessing." Mwindo answered, "Yes, my father." Muisa recollected: "Let them give a chair to Mwindo to sit on it."[175] Mwindo answered him: "Not at all, my father, even though a man is a guest, is that a reason for him to sit down on the head of his father?" Muisa also said that he had left a gourd of beer here: "Let me pour you a bit." Mwindo said: "No, my father, even though a man is a guest, is that a reason for him to drink the urine of his father?"[176] Muisa said: "Blessing, blessing, my father." Muisa again said: "Let them prepare some paste for you, oh Mwindo!" Mwindo answered him: "No, my father, even though a man is a guest, is that a reason for him to eat the excrements of his father?" Hearing that, Muisa said to him: "Blessing, blessing, Mwindo." Seeing Mwindo escape those ordeals, Muisa said to Mwindo: "Go and take a rest in the house there of your sister Kahindo."[177]

---

174. *tŏto/no, no*: onomatopoeia used to forbid children to do something; *kŏko/no* would be a more general term. Both expressions are accompanied by a gesture of prohibition. From the use of *tŏto*, it is once again clear that Mwindo looks like a child. Similar ordeals for testing shrewdness are currently found in Nyanga tales. *makangura / blessings*: the verb *įkangura* designates the action of pulling at one's limbs and fingers in a Nyanga gesture of blessing or of well-wishing.

175. *wísubukia / recollected*: the literal translation; the implication is that Muisa, stunned by his meeting with Mwindo, almost forgot to expose him to trickery, but reflected and then suddenly regained his self-control.

176. In the answers given by Mwindo, which were recommended by Muisa's daughter, Mwindo changes *mwana*, child, to *mwenį*, guest. The connotations of the terms are not far apart for *mwenį* designates a known guest who is related.

177. *your sister Kahindo*: the implication is not that Mwindo is related to her but rather that both are of about the same age.

Mwindo went inside. When he arrived in Kahindo's house, he looked around in it; he saw Kahindo inside the house; Kahindo had made herself like the anus of a snail in dressing up and in rubbing herself with red powder and castor oil. Mwindo, seeing her, was about to step back because of seeing sunbeams inside the house. Kahindo, seeing him, said to him: "Come in, oh Mwindo!"[178] Mwindo said: "May the one who remains behind hurt himself, oh my sister!" When she saw that Mwindo had entered into the house, she said to herself: "Lo!, Mwindo has hunger." She got up, she went to make some paste, "a little like that," of ashes.[179] After she had stirred it, she brought it to Mwindo in her sacred hut.[180] When Muisa saw Kahindo bringing (the paste) to Mwindo, he dashed quickly toward the house of his daughter; he went to spy where Mwindo was. He said to Mwindo: "Oh, my father Mwindo, you are eating this food; tomorrow, as soon as you are up and about, you will start cultivating a new banana grove for me; may you first cut leaves, then plant the banana trees, then fell the trees; may you then cut the newly grown weeds, then prune the banana trees, then prop them up, then bring ripe bananas. It's after you will have performed all those works that I shall know to give you your father."[181] After Muisa had spoken like that to Mwindo, he also said to him: "When you leave for cultivating, I

178. *had made herself like the anus of a snail*: i.e., was very clean, *karíbu/come in*: derived from Swahili. It is not a Nyanga custom to use such expressions when one wants to enter a house. If someone asks to come in, the person inside the house simply says *aé/yes*.

179. *wásitaré/may [he] hurt himself*: Mwindo's answer can only be understood in terms of the confusion the narrator had deliberately created between the Swahili word *astarehe* (which the Nyanga pronounce as *sitarehe)* and the Nyanga verb *isitara*, to injure oneself or to knock against. In Swahili custom, the visitor answers *astarehe* (be at rest!) when the person inside the house has permitted him to come in. *túrehĕ mpe/a little like that*: this expression is accompanied by a gesture. *A paste made of ashes*: this is the mythical food of Muisa, who lives in cold ashes.

180. *jremeso/sacred hut*: an oval-shaped hut dedicated by the Nyanga as a shrine to the spirit Kahombo. Nyanga men, who are ritually married to the spirit Kahombo, spend part of their time in it in the domestic cycle of living alternately with different wives. They also receive their guests in the hut.

181. Muisa rapidly enumerates the basic steps of banana-growing, using an extremely precise technical vocabulary, *úsekí na tó/then prop them up*: *tó* (them, used in connection with *esâmpókó*, banana trees) is grammatically incorrect. The correct form *só* is always avoided by the Nyanga, because it is also the term for "your father." The patterns of euphemistic speech compel the avoidance of the ambiguous usage of this word. *he went to spy*: it is considered bad for a father to spy on his unmarried daughter.

shall give you a man to observe the way in which you are performing the cultivation." After he had spoken like that, he left the doorway; he returned to his meeting place. Where Mwindo was sitting in the house, he started eating the paste. When the sky had become daylight, in the morning, Mwindo equipped himself with his billhook; Mwindo went to cultivate. Muisa picked out one man (who) accompanied Mwindo going to the fields. When they arrived in the forest, the man whom Muisa had picked out showed Mwindo a mountain with mango trees on it. Mwindo, seeing that mountain, placed the billhooks on the ground; all by themselves, they laid out the fresh trails.[182] Having finished the trail, they cut the grasses. Having cut the grasses, the banana trees planted themselves; the banana trees having planted themselves, Mwindo sent a bunch of axes down on them; the axes by themselves finished felling the trees. Finishing there, he sent a bunch of billhooks down on it; those billhooks went across the banana grove cutting the newly grown weeds.[183] Where the companion of Mwindo was sitting, he returned to Muisa. When he arrived there, he brought Muisa the news, saying: "This time he there is not (merely) a cultivator; he is fast, a cultivator of marvelous things; he has not touched one iron tool; the iron tools themselves are cultivating—and felling trees and cutting weeds." Having given the news, he returned again where Mwindo was on the fresh banana field. Where Mwindo was, the billhooks having finished cutting their weeds, they now cut gaffs; the gaffs themselves propped up the banana trees. The gaffs having finished sustaining the trees, the banana stems were ripe. The companion ran to bring the news to Muisa. He arrived there and said to Muisa: "It is not a man who is there; he has cultivated today; the banana trees already have stems and the bananas already (are) ripe."[184] He also said to Muisa that

182. *mango trees*: i.e., trees hard to fell, *mikandé/fresh trails*: when planting a new banana grove, the Nyanga first clear two narrow trails that stand perpendicular to each other, then they cut the brush in such a way as to form the third side of a triangle with the cut grasses.

183. The various sequences of agricultural activities are correctly described: the Nyanga fell the trees *after* planting the stipes; they do not burn.

184. This, like the preceding passage, is exceptionally precise in the use of technical terms and in the correct description of labor sequences, for example, *n'esâmbú íyé mbuÿa na/and the bananas already are ripe: mbú* is the generic term for edible bananas, *mbuÿa* the generic term for any ripe banana.

Mwindo was already on his way (with) that stem of bananas. Hearing this, Muisa said: "Lo! this boy here will (manage to) get through again there in the forest; I went to sleep after having deceived him in the evening, (but) he got himself loose; he has escaped that danger; and today I have again tested him, (but) here he is about to escape again." Having thus been astonished (because of) Mwindo, Muisa sent his *karemba*-belt of cowries over there; he said to it: "You, my *karemba*, you are going to Mwindo; when you will have seen him, you will have to bend him, then you will have to smash his mouth against the ground." *Karemba*, having heard the way in which it had been instructed by its master, went to the banana grove. When it saw Mwindo in the banana grove cutting up the banana stems on which there were ripe bananas, it went to where he was; it fell upon him where he was; it made Mwindo scream; it crushed him; it planted his mouth against the ground—froth came out; he lacked the way of getting his breath out; urine and excrements agreed (to get out); they lacked the one who could remove them. Having seen its master missing all means of getting out, Mwindo's *conga* recalled (its duty); it wagged itself above the head of Mwindo; Mwindo succeeded in sneezing; he raised his eyes upward; he opened his eyes; he raised them; he gazed about a little. After Mwindo had been wedged by Muisa's *karemba*, the rope became still, it did not move any more. Where his aunt had remained in Tubondo, where she had held one end of the rope, she threw herself down saying that lo! her son was dead. She uttered a cry, low and high, imploring the divinities, she said: "It is the one who will escape there who is (my) child."[185] Where Mwindo was, when he lifted up (his) eyes, he sang:

> Muisa slaughtered Mwindo,
> I shall die, oh Bira!

185. The narrator first describes fully in colorful language what happens to Mwindo: how he is beaten by Muisa's belt and saved by his *conga*-scepter. He then turns to the effects that Mwindo's seeming death had upon his aunt. *She threw herself down*: a normal manifestation of sorrow. *émuréngé émwįhį némore/a cry, low and high*: lit., a cry, nearby and far, or a cry, short and long. This expression is currently used to say that one does his best, exhausts all means. *It is the one who will escape there who is (my) child*: in her imploration to the divinities, the aunt means to say that in whatever shape Mwindo may return to her after this beating, she will care for him.

> Muisa, you are helpless against Mwindo,
> Against Mwindo, the Little-one-just-born-he-has-walked.

Mwindo, while singing, remembered his aunt: "You there in Tubondo, I had already felt that my rope did not move, that it had become still because Muisa had already wedged me; he had wrapped me up like a bunch of bananas; but don't suffer from anxiety any more, there where you are, because my hope has just warned you (that) I am saved. It is my *conga* that set me up again." Having reported the news to his aunt in recollecting her, Mwindo now sent his *conga* to Muisa in the village, saying: "You, my *conga*, when you will have arrived where Muisa is in the village, you will have to smash him with force; you must plant his mouth to the ground; his tongue must penetrate inside the earth; so long as I shall not be back, so long as I shall not have come there into the village, you should not have released him again." The *conga* went whirling around; when it arrived at Muisa's meeting place, it smashed him; it planted his mouth to the ground; the tongue dug into the earth; urine and excrements lacked *mpunga*-leaves, and the one who would take them away was also missing; breath found no way of coming out.[186] Where Mwindo remained in the banana grove, he prepared a load of green bananas together with ripe bananas. He returned to the village. When he cast his eyes at the meeting place, he saw Muisa—foam had come out of his mouth and nostrils. Kahindo, Muisa's daughter, seeing Mwindo, hurried to the place where he was; she told him: "You are arriving, whereas my father here has already cooled off." Mwindo answered Kahindo that he had come here looking for his father: "Now give me my father here, so that I may go home with him." Kahindo answered him: "Begin first by healing my father, so that I know how to unveil your father, so that I may give him to you." Mwindo sang while awakening Muisa:

---

186. *ịsịrị/anxiety*: lit., bad omens. The passage implies that Iyangura and Mwindo are not only linked by a liana, but that there is some kind of mystical, telepathic bond between them for Mwindo is said to inform his aunt about his salvation by merely thinking about her (*wásubukia, mwímumbukia*). The paternal aunt who acts as an advisor is the protagonist in Nyanga dreams. Tales frequently suggest that persons lost in the forest hear the voice of their paternal aunt (represented as a reed flute, *mpingú*) giving advice and warnings, *mpunga-leaves*: the Nyanga version of toilet paper.

He who went to sleep wakes up.
Muisa, you are powerless against Mwindo,
Because Mwindo (is) the Little-one-just-born-he-walked.
Kahombo, whom Muisa brought forth,
He-who-is-accustomed-to-mocking-himself.
Muisa, you are helpless against Mwindo.
A bit of food, thanks, puts an end to a song.[187]

Mwindo went on singing like that while beating Muisa incessantly on the head with his *conga* in order to wake him up. When Musia had awakened, when he was safe, he said: "You, Mwindo, lo! you also are a man." Muisa also said to Mwindo: "You, child, go as soon as you are awake to extract for me my honey which is in that tree there." Mwindo complained: "This time I am dead once more."[188] After Mwindo had been shown that honey by Muisa so as to set out in the early morning to extract (it), sky became night. Kahindo stirred paste for Mwindo; Mwindo ate it. Having eaten the paste, they went to partake in sleep. When the sky had become day, in the morning, Mwindo provided himself with his axe; he went ahead into the forest to extract the honey; he also took fire. When he arrived at the base of the tree, he climbed (up into) the tree; he went to arrive at the fascicle where the honey was; he called: "Is this the place?" They answered him: "There it is; 'Lo! he will be able to handle it.'" Mwindo poked up the fire for it. He struck his axe at the tree; he sang:

I am extracting honey in Muisa's (country);
Kabumbu-woodpecker is hanging in the high emptiness.
Women-who-are-lingering-on-the-other-side-of-the river,
    listen (to)
The way in which the little female forger of words is
    speaking.[189]

---

187. *ịsịsa/cool off*: like food; euphemistic for to die. *A bit of food, thanks, puts an end to a song*: the narrator is invited to go to eat and thanks his host.

188. *wáhend'ịkundo/ go as soon as you are awake to extract honey*: the verb *jhónda* followed by verbs like to eat, to go, and so on, designates an activity undertaken in the early morning, shortly after awakening. *nakwịré/I am dead*: complaint currently uttered by women to express suffering, hardship.

189. *they went to partake in sleep*: the context (she prepared food for him) and the form *bénda* (they went) seem to imply that Mwindo slept with Kahindo, although it

My friend Nkuba, may you be victorious.
Hatred is in the heart.
My little father threw me into the drum into the river;
My father believed that I would fade away.

Where Muisa remained in the village, he said: "Lo! this man will finally extract this honey!" Muisa sent his *karemba*-belt; it went and smashed Mwindo on the tree; it planted his mouth into the trunk of the tree; his breath could not get out; urine and excrements trickled down from him.

Where his aunt Iyangura was, the rope reminded her, she said that lo! her son was dead. This rope had again become still. Where Mwindo (had) left his *conga* down on the ground, the *conga* realized that lo! its master was dead; it climbed up where he was; it went to beat and beat on the head of Mwindo. Mwindo sneezed; he lifted his eyes and a bit of breath came out. Mwindo said: "Lo! while I was perched, lo! I was on the verge of death." When he had opened his eyes, he implored his friend Nkuba; he sang:

My friend Nkuba, be victorious.
Hatred is in the heart.

In climbing down (from the tree), he implored Nkuba, he gazed into the sky: "My friend Nkuba, I am suffering." When Nkuba heard the cry of his friend Mwindo, he came down onto the tree; he cleaved it into pieces. His friend Mwindo went down, (but) he did not have a single wound. When he was down with the basket of honey, he went up to Muisa's with the honey. He arrived there; he placed the honey basket down for him saying that there was the honey, but that he wanted him to give him his father. Muisa hearing this sent a boy to look for the place where he had hidden Shemwindo. The boy arrived there whereas Shemwindo was no longer there; lo! it was Muisa who

---

would have been normal and less ambiguous to add euphemistic expressions for the idea of having intercourse. *wákúmányie kashá/poked up the fire*: the verbal phrase describes literally Mwindo putting pieces of dried wood and leaves together, burning them in order to smoke out the bees. *Kabumbu-woodpecker is hanging in the high emptiness*: Mwindo compares himself to the toughness of the woodpecker who makes holes in the trees, *nya-késj kábinwa/the little female forger of words*: women who are talkative, but speak skillfully, receive this epithet.

had warned Shemwindo that he should flee to Ntumba's. Having looked for the place where Shemwindo had hidden himself, and having seen that there was no one there, the boy returned to Muisa and Mwindo; he arrived there; he told them: "You, you are sitting here (while) Shemwindo has fled; he is not in the place where he was (before)." Kahungu came; he gave Mwindo the news: "Your companion Muisa lies; it is he who has warned your father to flee to Ntumba's, saying that you are too tough."[190] After Kahungu had told Mwindo the news in that manner, he flew away into the sky. Where Mwindo and Muisa remained, Mwindo told him the truth bluntly. "Give me my father on the shot. Make him come out from where you have hidden him so that I may go with him; oh! you are like that, (are you) you scoundrel? You (had) said that when I would have cultivated a field for you, when I would have extracted honey for you, you would then give me my father. I want you to take him out right now; don't let the saliva dry up without having taken him out." When Muisa heard how Mwindo was criticizing him, he twitched his eyes; he said: "This time, this boy makes my belly swell here in my own village."[191]

Having seen that Muisa did not bring his father out, Mwindo beat Muisa on top of his head with his *conga*; Muisa, excrements stuck to the buttocks; he fainted away; urine ran all over the ground; froth came out from his nose and eyes (and) covered his face; he tossed his hoofs up into the air; he stiffened like a *mukusa*-viper.[192] Mwindo said: "Stay like that, you dog"; he would heal him when he would be back from where he was going. Mwindo went in pursuit of his father, where he had gone to Ntumba's. Mwindo went on singing:

190. Although the verbal forms used here leave some uncertainty, it seems quite sure that in this and the preceding passages neither Mwindo nor Muisa really die; the verb *jnjnke* means to faint, and *ikurá*, as well as meaning to die, covers a broad range of sufferings. The verb *ihúhúka*, to draw the last breath, which is not used here, would clearly have signified that they were really dead. It may be assumed that they were in a kind of deep sleep, a torpor, unconscious because of the beatings they had received. *Ntumba* is a personification of the aardvark, a rare and sacred animal for the Nyanga.

191. *this boy makes my belly swell*: i.e., is a serious nuisance. The expression is related to the drinking of poison during ordeals.

192. *wáhúhúka/he fainted away*: the verbal form used here and the description (*he tossed his hoofs up . . ., he stiffened*) means that Muisa really dies.

I am searching for Shemwindo
In the place where Shemwindo went.
Shemwindo fled into Ntumba's dwelling,
Into Muisa's dwelling.
I am searching for Ntumba's dwelling,
For Munundu's dwelling.
Ntumba, open for me.
Shemwindo has set a barrier inside Munundu's dwelling;
Shemwindo is in flight inside Ntumba's dwelling.
I am searching for my father Shemwindo
In Ntumba's, in Munundu's dwelling.
The sun sets down.
I am searching for Shemwindo;
Shemwindo is in flight inside Ntumba's dwelling,
Inside Munundu's.
My little father threw me into the drum.

Mwindo implored Nkuba, saying:

My friend Nkuba, may you be victorious.
Hatred is in the heart.
My little father, the dearest one,
I am searching for my father in Ntumba's dwelling,
In Munundu's.
My friend Nkuba, may you be victorious,
Hatred is in the heart.
I am looking for my little father, the dearest one.
My little father threw me into the drum,
My little father, eternal malefactor among people.
My little father shot me into the river.[193]
Ntumba, open for me,
I am looking for my little father, the dearest one.

---

193. *Munundu*: lit., the lair of an aardvark, but given here as an epithet for Ntumba, the aardvark. *katitá kashé-karúo/my father, the dearest one*: lit., my little father, the little possessor of the ladle. This is a common honorific term for father, but, as is clear from the context and also from the diminutive, pejorative ka- prefix, it is used sarcastically here, *kashémungó/eternal malefactor*: in Nyanga, the morpheme *shé-* (lit., his father) is employed in widely different contexts to indicate ownership, association, mastery, and control over. *kándása/shot me*: *irása* is to shoot an arrow.

While Mwindo was still pacing around Ntumba's cave where his father was, and Ntumba from the inside (at first) paid no attention (to him), then Ntumba made a sign to Shemwindo, saying: "You be ready to go; the little male at the door here is strong, and you are witnessing the way in which he is threatening at the entrance of the cave."[194] When Shemwindo heard the way in which his son toughened himself at the entrance of the cave, he said: "The little boy comes (to us) with severity." He said to his friend Ntumba that he was fleeing. Shemwindo went to escape to Sheburungu's. Where Nkuba was in the sky, when he heard the voice of his friend, he said: "My friend is already too tired of beseeching me." Nkuba sent down seven lightnings; they descended into Ntumba's cave; they cleaved it into a million pieces; the cave turned into mere dust; the dust flew up. Realizing that his friend Nkuba had cleft the cave, Mwindo opened the door; he entered the interior of the cave; he looked and looked for his father here and there inside the cave; he did not see him. He met Ntumba inside; he told him: "You, Ntumba, where did you let my father go, where have you hidden him?" Ntumba kept silent as though he had not heard. Mwindo spit saliva at him, saying: "Get out, you scoundrel! Lo! (while) I was laboring at the door asking that you open for me, you refused. May you die of scrotal elephantiasis." When Ntumba witnessed the way in which Mwindo continued blaming him because of his father, saying that he had made him flee, he said to Mwindo: "You see how my house was just destroyed and all my crops; what shall I do then?" Mwindo said: "You are crazy; don't make me smell your breath where I am! So! that's what you are like!" Where Kahungu dwelt in the sky, he came down; he went to bring the news to Mwindo; he arrived saying: "You know, you Mwindo, that Ntumba has made your father escape; your father has fled to Sheburungu's." Kahungu, having brought Mwindo the news again, flew away into the sky. Where Mwindo remained at Ntumba's—because of anger and weariness—he said to Ntumba: "You Ntumba, that is the (death) you will die; may you never again find food in this country of yours." Having spoken to him in that way, he went to where his father had gone; he went in search of him. Where his aunt Iyangura dwelt in Tubondo, she went on pondering sadly saying: "My heart will be back only when Mwindo will be back from

---

194. *kákarámá/is strong: ikarama*, to harden an animal hide by drying it in the sun.

where he has gone."[195] She looked at the rope that she was holding; she said: "Lo! Mwindo is still going in search of the place where his father went." Where Mwindo continued to follow his father, going in search of him all wrapped up in hatred, he went to arrive at the entrance of Sheburungu's village. He met little children there; they greeted him, saying: "Are you awake, oh Mwindo?"[196] Mwindo answered them: "Yes." After the youngsters had greeted Mwindo, they told him: "You, Mwindo, don't draw ahead of us; we are hungry; we ask you for food." Mwindo implored his aunt Iyangura to send him food (telling her) that the children of Sheburungu were hungry. While asking for food from his aunt, Mwindo sang. Mwindo howled, he said:

> Oh! father, where Iyangura remained,
> Sister of Shemwindo,
> I claim seven portions (of food).[197]
> You see where Mwindo passed,
> I am suffering from hunger.
> Aunt Iyangura,
> I am claiming meat.

Mwindo had spoken in that way:

> I claim seven portions (of food).
> You see that I woke up and set out on my journey.
> Where my aunt remained,
> Again I claim seven portions (of food).
> Aunt, I have expressed my desire for meat.

Having implored his aunt, saying that he wanted seven pastes with meat to join him in the place where he was with the children of Sheburungu, when Mwindo looked up, the pastes were already there, having come from his aunt Iyangura. After the food had arrived, Mwindo gave it to the youngsters. The children of Sheburungu began eating the paste, while Mwindo was keeping company with them.[198] When the

195. *Sheburungu*: commonly one of the epithets given to the creator god Ongo.

196. *ébusíbúké bútí nti wákumukanda/[Mwindo was] all wrapped up in hatred*: in the Nyanga text hatred is personified, i.e., hatred literally made a package of Mwindo.

197. *bishá/portions of food*: lit., the complete, untouched contents of a plate.

198. *nti watékésá bo/he was keeping company with them*: lit., to be a mere onlooker while others eat. The idea of nonparticipation in a specific activity is expressed by many different Nyanga verbs.

children had finished eating, Mwindo returned the wicker plates to his aunt Iyangura, saying to line them up in order for him to be able to climb up to Sheburungu's, the household utensils having finished returning.[199] Mwindo sent back the wicker plates, singing:

> I send back the wicker and wooden plates.
> Oh! Aunt Iyangura,[200]
> I send back the wicker and wooden plates.

After he had sent back the wicker and wooden plates, he proceeded to climb up to Sheburungu's, and the youngsters followed him.[201] He went up to Sheburungu's, singing:

> Sheburungu, you,
> I am looking for Shemwindo.
> Shemwindo gave birth to a hero
> In giving birth to the Little-one-just-born-he-walked.
> Sheburungu,
> I am looking for Shemwindo,
> My little father, the dearest one.

Sheburungu shouted and said:

> Oh Mwindo, let us play *wiki* together![202]

199. It is altogether normal for Mwindo to insist on returning the dishes to his mother before he continues his search for his father. It is a strict custom among the Nyanga to return all empty plates to their places immediately after the meal is finished. Nyanga men eat together, separately from their wives and young children; in the men's hut they share the various meals prepared by their respective wives. As soon as they are finished eating, the empty plates are sent back to their wives' houses for fear that ill-inspired sorcerers may use the remaining food particles against them. A housewife is always uneasy so long as the plates have not been returned.

200. *Mahíme/oh!*: the meaning of this expression varies according to its tones and the context in which it occurs. It introduces a question: Is it not true? Don't you agree? It stands at the beginning of an imploration: Pity! Mercy! It is used in arguments to say: you are my witness.

201. It is customary for children playing at the outskirts of the village to follow arriving visitors. Moreover, Mwindo himself has the appearance of a child.

202. *túresé/let us play wiki: ịresa* means to gamble, it refers to any kind of game that involves an element of chance and in which various goods are staked. The game in which enemies most frequently challenge each other in Nyanga tales is that of *wiki* (handfuls of little black seed are taken with the object of guessing the number of seeds held in each hand). In daily life, this game is played only by men, who often wager large amounts of possessions.

And Mwindo shouted and said:

> Oh! my father Sheburungu,
> I am looking for Shemwindo.

And he—

> Oh Mwindo, let us play *wiki* together!

And Mwindo shouted, he said:

> Oh my father, give me Shemwindo!
> My little father threw me into the drum;
> My little father threw me into the river.
> The youngsters asked me to play *wiki* with them,
> The youngsters—I do not play *wiki* with them.

After Mwindo had entreated Sheburungu, asking him to give him back his father, Sheburungu said to him: "I cannot give you your father; I am asking that we first play *wiki* together, so that I may deliver your father to you, so that you may go home with him." After Sheburungu had spoken like that to Mwindo, Mwindo answered him: "Spread them (the *wiki*) out on the ground; I will not flee from you; you know the dangers from which I have escaped."[203] After Sheburungu had heard the way in which he was being answered by Mwindo, he went to fetch a mat; he spread it out on the ground; he also went to get the very old *wiki*-seeds of the *isea*-tree. Sheburungu wagered: "You, Mwindo, if you beat me, you will carry your father off (with you), and here (are) three bunches of *butea*-money; if you beat me, you will carry them off." Mwindo wagered three bunches of *butea*-money. After they had wagered things with each other in that way, Sheburungu was the first to take a handful of *wiki*-seeds; when he picked them up, with the first take-up, he won Mwindo's *butea*-money. Mwindo wagered the goats that remained in Tubondo; Sheburungu took the *wiki*- seeds; he won all the goats from Mwindo. Mwindo wagered everything and his aunt; Sheburungu again took the seeds; he won all the goods and the people and his aunt from Mwindo.[204] Mwindo remained all alone with his *conga*, his partner

---

203. *byámoswá we/which I have escaped: joswa* literally means to be left with only the feathers of the bird one is trying to catch.

204. In this *wiki* game men would wager all their possessions, including wives and daughters.

Sheburungu having finished winning from him all the things and all the people who lived in Tubondo. After Mwindo had been losing all his things and his people, he wagered his *conga*. When Sheburungu tried to take the seeds, he failed. Mwindo took the seeds; he won from Sheburungu the money that he had wagered. Sheburungu wagered again; Mwindo again took the seeds; he won on eight; all that Sheburungu had wagered, Mwindo won it back.[205] Sheburungu wagered all his objects, together with his cattle. Mwindo took the seeds up again; he won again on eight; he won all the things of Sheburungu: people, goats, cattle. Mwindo piled up (things); Sheburungu remained all alone by himself.

Where Kantori and Kahungu remained, they arrived where Mwindo was; they warned him: "You, Mwindo, come quickly; your father wants to flee again." After he had heard that news, Mwindo abondoned the *wiki*-game; he headed very quickly to join his father in the banana grove of Sheburungu. Seeing him, they put their nails into him.[206] Seeing his father, Mwindo inquired of him: "Oh my father, is it you here?" Shemwindo answered: "Here I am." Mwindo again inquired of his father: "Oh Shemwindo, is it really you?" Shemwindo again answered: "Here I am, you, my son." After Mwindo had seized his father like that, he returned with him; he climbed up with him to Sheburungu's. Mwindo said to Sheburungu: "You, Sheburungu, you have been hiding my father away. This one here is my father, is he not?" Mwindo said further to Sheburungu: "You, Sheburungu, I don't want any of your things that I have won; now keep all your things that I have won; here I am going with my father." When he was about to return with his father, Mwindo gave his farewell to Sheburungu and to all his people: "Oh, my father Sheburungu, farewell!" Sheburungu answered: "Yes, you too, Mwindo, go and be strong, along with your father

205. *mináni/eight*: to be understood as "at the count of eight."
206. *kisambú/banana grove*: the term designates a banana grove in full production with many banana trees and interspersed with many other crops. *bámuhára mó byára/ they put their nails into him*: *thára* literally means to scratch; the stereotyped expression is used in connection with catching thieves or with arresting someone who resists. The verbal form signifies that Mwindo himself does not lay hands on his father; his followers, in fact, had remained back in the village. "They" may be a rare *plurale majestatis* for "he" or may stand for the young children whom Mwindo had met at the entrance of Sheburungu's village.

Shemwindo." After Mwindo had said farewell to Sheburungu, he returned singing:

> Listen, Ntumba Munundu,[207]
> He who went (away) comes back.

Mwindo shook the rope, he reminded his aunt; and where his aunt remained, she had bells attached to the rope. Mwindo sang:

> He who went (away) comes back;
> You see I am carrying Shemwindo.[208]

Mwindo rushed headlong to Ntumba's cave; he arrived there when Ntumba had already finished rebuilding (it). Mwindo sang:

> I am longing for Ntumba Munundu's.
> The country is a *mutaka*-fish.[209]
> He who went to sleep wakes up.

Mwindo said to Ntumba: "Why did you hide my father away? Here I am with my father." Mwindo sang:

> Ntumba, you are powerless against Mwindo,
> For Mwindo is the Little-one-just-born-he-has-walked.
> I am on my way home from this point on in Ntumba's house.

---

207 The dignified attitude of mutual respect with which father and son treat each other is truly impressive: no fighting, no slander. Mwindo's encounter with his father has a cathartic effect on him; from now on Mwindo is in a reconciliatory mood. The attitude attributed to Mwindo is in line with the Nyanga code of values: the ideal man is not subject to verbosity, rancor; he does not manifest excessive emotions. It is only from the moment of his encounter with his father that Mwindo demonstrates his true greatness. *Rúkira waNtúmba/listen, Ntumba*: the connective form *wa-* occurs here as a kind of synonym of *muna-* with the rare meaning of master or of the kind, species of.

208. *niríte/I am carrying*: here, the meaning is unclear. The verbal form *niríte* can mean that Mwindo really carries his father on his back, or that he is simply in the company of his father, that he has his father with him. *niríte* is often used in the latter sense, e.g., when one says *niríte mpéné* or *niríte kikumí*, I have a goat or I have a nubile daughter.

209. *écŭo mutáká/the country is a mutaka-fish*: the interpretation of *mutáká* is difficult; said with one low and two high tones, the word designates a little fish with red stripes, which is a symbol of beauty. The meaning would then be: the country is beautiful, *mutaka* with three low tones means landed estate. This interpretation is also possible if we accept tonal change owing to the rhythm of the song. In this case, the meaning would be that there is no state or political unit without land, i.e., a group cannot have political autonomy if it is not in full control of the land.

Look, I am carrying Shemwindo,
My little father, the dearest-one,
Shemwindo, senior brother of Iyangura.
It is Shemwindo, the one who gave birth to a hero.
Aunt Iyangura, I am on my way back.
Mwindo is the Little-one-just-born-he-walked.
I am carrying my little father, Shemwindo.
Katakwa-region, lowland intersected with flooding streams.[210]
You see, I went to give allegiance to the Baniyana.

When Mwindo arrived at Ntumba's, he related the whole story to
Ntumba; he said to him: "You, Ntumba, you were wrong to offend me
in vain." All the things of Ntumba, the land, and the banana groves,
and the people, everything came back. Mwindo and his father
Shemwindo spent the night at Ntumba's. After Mwindo had saved all
the things of Ntumba, Ntumba said to Mwindo: "Go, you senior, I
never utter slander against you; I have no dispute with you." When
Mwindo left Ntumba's, together with his father, he went singing,
reminding his aunt in Tubondo:

He who has gone away is back.
Muisa!
The sky has become day.[211]
The rooster cock-a-doodle-dooed,[212]
And the sparrow pointed him out.
Mwindo will arrive in the house of Muisa,
In the house of Nyarire;
I come from Ntumba's,
From Munundu's.
Muisa, you are helpless against Mwindo,
Since Mwindo is the Little-one-just-born-he-has-walked.
It is you who are wrong in offending me in vain.

---

210. *Katakwa*: an area in Nyanga country known for its rich fishing; the rivers there
flood very often leaving small pools and channels full of water and fish where the
Nyanga set up weirs and traps. This verse, which is thrown in by the narrator, is freely
translated in the spirit of what is meant here and what we were able to observe at the
moment it was uttered. It could be handled as: *Katakwá* (region), *kumbo* (downstream),
mikómbị (flooding rivers).

211. *wácere/has become day*: the Nyangaized Hunde form *bwakyére*.

212. *birangira/cock-a-doodle-dooed*: onomatopoeia borrowed from Hunde.

Look! I am carrying Shemwindo.
Muisa, you are helpless against Mwindo,
Since Mwindo is the Little-one-just-born-he-walked.
Look! I am carrying Shemwindo.
I am returning to Tubondo,
Where remained my aunt Iyangura,
Iyangura, sister of Shemwindo,
Aunt, birth-giver, Iyangura.[213]
I shall eat on the wicker and wooden plates
Only when I shall arrive in Tubondo.[214]

When Mwindo left Ntumba's village with his father Shemwindo, he went headlong into Muisa's house. When Mwindo was already in Muisa's house, Kahindo came to Mwindo saying: "You see my father here, his bones fill a basket; what shall I do then? It is befitting that you heal my father; don't leave him like that; wake him up, may my father wake up, because he is the chief of all the people." After Kahindo had spoken to Mwindo in that way, Mwindo woke up Muisa singing:

He who went to sleep wakes up,
My father Muisa,
He who went to sleep wakes up.
Look!
You,
It is you who have offended me in vain.
Look!
I am carrying my father Shemwindo.
Muisa,
He who went to sleep wakes up.
Muisa,

213. *Nyarire*: contracted form for Nyamurairi, the god of fire who heads all other divinities. Mwindo did not meet with Nyarire, but with one of his servants, Muisa. *ngí muhemúké/who are wrong in offending me*: *ihemuka* literally means not to give to those who ask; *ngí* (it is) underlines the fact that the injustice of their action is now very clear, *kabúto/birth-giver*: an epithet for a paternal aunt or a father; interestingly, this epithet is not given to a mother. It underscores the importance of the patrilineal ideology in which a paternal aunt is a closer relative than a mother. *kabúto* literally means the action (suffix *-o*) of giving birth, or, rather, of perpetuating patrilineal kinship.

214. The suggestion is clear that Mwindo does not eat during his various peregrinations.

You are helpless against Mwindo,
Mwindo is the Little-one-just-born-he-walked.
Shemwindo brought forth a hero.
I am going to Aunt Iyangura's village,
Iyangura, sister of Shemwindo.

While Mwindo was awakening Muisa, he kept on striking him all the time with his *conga*, telling him: "You have offended me in vain; you have tried to be equal to Mwindo, whereas Mwindo is the Little-one-just-born-he-walked, the little one who does not eat terrestrial foods; and the day he was born, he did not drink at the breasts of his mother." When Mwindo had finished waking up Muisa, Muisa woke up, he resuscitated. After Muisa had resuscitated, Mwindo told him that he had been forged by his uncles, the Baniyana. "My body is covered with iron only; and you, Muisa, don't you see me? Is that why you mounted me?" Muisa asked Mwindo: "You, Mwindo, how were you born? Do you have a medicine that enables your going?" Mwindo unfolded for him the thread of the news of how he was born. He told him: "You, Muisa, lo! have you never heard that I came out of the medius of my mother, that I was not born in the same way that other children are born, that I was born speaking and even walking? You, Muisa, have you never heard that I was thrown into a grave, that they had even put banana stems on it, that I resuscitated again, that my father threw me anew into the drum, that he threw me into the river, that I came out of it again? Have you not heard all these marvelous things, you, Muisa? That is why you dared to make a fool of me."

When Mwindo was already at Muisa's, he agitated the rope where his aunt remained in Tubondo; he reminded her. Iyangura said to Mwindo's uncles, the Baniyana, that in the place where Mwindo had gone, he had long ago finished seizing his father, that he was on his way home with him. While returning to Tubondo, Mwindo said farewell to Muisa; he sang:

You, Muisa,
You see me already going,
You, Muisa, taker of others' things.
Where Aunt Iyangura remains
In Tubondo,
He who went away is back.

When Muisa saw Mwindo going, he said to him: "Oh, Mwindo, you my son, it's befitting that you marry my Kahindo here." Mwindo answered him: "I cannot marry here; I shall marry (later) in Tubondo of Shemwindo."

In leaving Muisa's village, Mwindo began the trip; he and his father went home; they went to appear where they had entered at the root of the *kikoka*-fern. When Mwindo and Shemwindo arrived at the entrance of Tubondo, those who were in the village, Iyangura and the uncles of Mwindo, swarmed in the village like bees; they went to greet Mwindo and his father at the entrance; they met them.[215] Seeing Mwindo, Iyangura and the uncles of Mwindo lifted him up into the air; they carried him on their fingertips. When they traversed the village of Tubondo, Mwindo told them to let him down. They put him down in the middle of the village place; they went to take a lot of spearheads, and it is on them that Mwindo sat down—they stood for the *utebe*-stool. His maternal uncles put him to the test like that in order to know if perhaps their nephew was still as they (had) forged him. When Mwindo was on the stool in the middle of the village, he gave his aunt the news from where he had come and the way in which he had fought, searching for his father. He sang:

When I descended with the rope,
Aunt,
I met with Kahindo.
Kahindo shouted (and) said:
"Mwindo, let me charge you with (the following) words:
If you see Muisa,
What Muisa will say,
You should refuse it."
Mwindo said:
"I go to the village, the village place
Where Muisa lives,
If I am not victorious
Where Muisa remains."

215. *umushata mó/you dared to make a fool of me: ishata* literally means to play, to make a game of. *bárubuka ... bírí mintsuntsu/they swarmed like bees*: the verb *irubuka* describes the sudden appearance of a swarm of bees or the way in which clear water is troubled when a stone is thrown into it

When I arrived in the village of Muisa,
Muisa shouted and said:
—Muisa brought out a chair—
"Mwindo, sit down here."
Mwindo shouted, complaining,
Saying, "This is your head, Muisa."
Muisa shouted and said:
"Counselors, give me some little beer
So that I may give it to Mwindo."
And Mwindo shouted, complaining:
"A father's urine a child never drinks."
Muisa said: "Let us fight together."
I have kneaded Muisa.
I was already going.[216]
I arrived in Ntumba's cave,
In the cave of Ntumba Munundu.
Ntumba said: "Let's fight together."
I kneaded Ntumba,
I who had kneaded Muisa.
You too, Ntumba, are powerless against Mwindo,
Mwindo, the Little-one-just-born-he-walked.
I kneaded Ntumba so that I got tired.
Already I was hurrying in Sheburungu's house;
When I arrived there at the entrance of Sheburungu's—
        a god—[217]

216. *bámukųkųma/they lifted him up*: this is commonly done to honor somebody. *shįnga/rope*: Swahili word. Earlier the line connecting him with his aunt was called *murí* (liana), *kumbúka kubutara/to the village, the village place*: the first term stands in opposition to the forest, the second one to the houses, *nará nendánge/I was going already*: typical expression meaning that he did not linger, that he hurried, and literally translated, would read: I set out to eat (while) going.

217. *kwáshé-Burúngú ongo/Sheburungu—a god*: the exact interpretation is difficult. Sheburungu is sometimes used as the epithet of Ongo, the creator god. But, judging from the fact that in the word order here, *ongo* follows *sheburungu*, it would seem that Mwindo is speaking about one of the Nyanga divinities and not about the creator god. For this reason *ongo* has not been written with a capital letter. As used here, *ongo* is somewhat synonymous with *mushumbú*, the generic term for divinity. Acceptable interpretations, then, are either "Sheburungu, one of the gods," or "Sheburungu, great as a god."

The youngsters howled, saying:
"Oh, Mwindo, we are hungry."
I sent pastes over there;
The youngsters ate the pastes.
Already I was on my way to Sheburungu's,
Together with the youngsters.
Sheburungu said: "Let us play *wiki* together."
I said: "You, Sheburungu,
You are powerless against Mwindo, the Little-one-just-
    born-he-walked.
Who made Muisa and Ntumba fail."
I shouted, complaining,
I, saying: "Give me my father here."
Sheburungu shouted, saying,
"Mwindo, you are helpless (in) the *wiki*-game against
    Sheburungu,
Which has beaten Heaven and Earth."[218]
We took a handful of *mbai*-seeds.
Mwindo shouted and said:
"Sheburungu, you are helpless against Mwindo.
Give me Shemwindo,
You see, I have already beaten you."
Kahungu notified Mwindo;
Kahungu showed me Shemwindo.
It is I who seized Shemwindo,
My little father, the dearest one.
We were already on the return trip;
"Shemwindo, let us go home,
Let us go up to Tubondo
Where remained Aunt Iyangura."
What Shemwindo accomplished!
I arrive at the peak in Tubondo.

---

218. *Bųtų́ n'Oto/Heaven and Earth*: both are personified here. I have not found these personifications elsewhere in Nyanga tales. The two verbs *jrésa* and *irása* used in the passage should not be confused: the first means to gamble (particularly to play the *wiki* game), the second means to shoot an arrow or to win a game.

You see, I am carrying Shemwindo;
I am carrying my little father, the dearest one.

Iyangura gave her son the order: "Since you have arrived with your father, bring him first into the *iremeso*-hut to let him rest there."[219] They carried Shemwindo into the *iremeso*-hut; he settled down in it. In giving hospitality to his father, Mwindo killed for him the goat that never defecates and never urinates; they cooked it, along with rice, for his father.[220] He said to his father: "Here are your goats! It is you who were wrong in vain; you made yourself awkward to Mwindo, the Little-one-just-born-he-walked, when you said that you did not want (any) boys, that you wanted girls; you did a deliberate wrong in the way you desired.[221] Lo! you did not know the strength of the blessing of Mwindo."[222] After Mwindo had given food to his father as a hospitality gift, Iyangura said to him: "You, my son, shall we go on living always in this desolate village, (we) alone, without other people? I, Iyangura, I want you first to save all the people who lived here in this village; when they have resuscitated, it is then only that I shall know to ask our young man, Shemwindo, to tell me some of the news of the ways in which he acted, all the evil that he did against you." Mwindo listened to the order of his aunt to heal those who had died. His uncles, the Baniyana, beat the drum for him while he, Mwindo, was dancing

219. *What Shemwindo accomplished!*: a shortened, euphemistic expression to say: the deed that Shemwindo accomplished is bad. *iremeso-hut*: an oval-shaped hut, which is also a shrine for the spirit of good fortune and a place in which guests are accommodated. The implication is that Shemwindo is no longer treated as a chief, the possessor of the village Tubondo, but merely as an important guest.

220. *the goat that never defecates and never urinates*: i.e., a very fat goat *mumpunge/rice*: a Nyangaized version of the Swahili word for growing rice, *mpunga*. Dry rice cultivation was introduced among the Nyanga in recent decades. The narrator speaks about rice, rather than about banana paste, to emphasize the fact that much effort was taken to prepare a fine meal for Mwindo. Rice-growing demands much more attention and maintenance than banana-growing. In addition, the Nyanga feel that it takes more time to prepare a rice porridge than a banana paste.

221. *uhemúkéngá/you were wrong*: said by someone who asks for a service and does not receive it; Mwindo criticizes his father's lack of generosity in this way.

222. *karamo kémukjsa/the strength of the blessing*: *karamo* refers to good health, long life, life force, and is used as a greeting. *mukjsa* means recovery from illness and is generally considered to be a blesssing of the spirits.

because of the joys of seeing his father. They sang. Aunt shouted and said:

My father, eternal savior of people.[223]

Mwindo said:

Oh, father, they tell me to save the people;
I say: "He who went to sleep wakes up."
Little Mwindo is the Little-one-just-born-he-walked.
My little father threw me into the drum.
Shemwindo, you do not know how to lead people.
The habits of people are difficult.
My little father, eternal malefactor among people,
Made bees fall down on me,
(Bees) of day and sun;
I lacked all means (of protection) against them.[224]

While Mwindo was healing those who died in Tubondo, he continued on in the (following) way: when he arrived at the bone of a man, he beat it with his *conga* so that the man would then wake up. The resuscitation was as follows:

each one who died in pregnancy resuscitated with her
     pregnancy;
each one who died in labor resuscitated being in labor;
each one who was preparing paste resuscitated stirring
     paste;
each one who died defecating resuscitated defecating;
each one who died setting up traps resuscitated trapping;
each one who died copulating resuscitated copulating;
each one who died forging resuscitated forging;
each one who died cultivating resuscitated cultivating;

223. *múmurárá úno/in this desolate village*: the image is that of a filthy village where the grasses are allowed to grow wild. *bushwá ésángoa síshé, serímusúnga/because of the joys of seeing his father*: the word order in Nyanga is reversed; lit., because of the joys of his father, (the joys) of seeing him. *shé karamo/eternal savior: she-* implies a special association of ownership, mastery, control; *karamo* is good health, long life, life force.

224. *yákịndị ná mwīshí/(bees) of day and sun*: stereotyped expression to say "all of a sudden." Mwindo is saying that his father suddenly and unexpectedly exposed him to all kinds of dangers.

each one who died while making pots and jars resuscitated
    shaping;
each one who died carving dishes resuscitated carving;
each one who died quarreling with a partner resuscitated
    quarreling.

Mwindo stayed in the village for three days resuscitating people; he was
dead of weariness. The people and all the houses—each person resuscitated being straight up in his house.[225] Tubondo filled itself again with
the people and the goats, the dogs, the cattle, the poultry, the male and
the female ewes, the teenage boys and girls, the children and the youngsters, the old males and females; in the middle of all those people (were)
the nobles and the counselors and the Pygmies and all the royal initiators; all those also were straight up. All the descent groups that formerly dwelt in Tubondo resuscitated; again they became as they were
before, each person who died having things of a certain quantity, resuscitated still having his things.[226] Tubondo again became a big village

225. *mwifúca bó bo/the resuscitation was as follows*: lit., while revivifying them in
this way. *bikango/weariness*: weakness caused by extreme physical strain, *kíra/each*:
Nyangaized Swahili word, *kila* (each). *wíhandá na múmwe/being straight up in his
house*: lit., planting himself (like a tree) in his (place or house).
226. The enumeration of animals and people who reoccupied the village of
Tubondo is succinct and precise. Listed are the various categories of domestic animals
traditionally known by the Nyanga: goats, sheep, chickens, dogs. Cattle *(nkambú)*,
although they are not traditional and were not found in Nyanga country at the time this
text was taken down, are mentioned in this section of the epic. There are various reasons
accountable for the inclusion of cattle: the narrator's imagination (he had been traveling
and working in neighboring areas), the presence of cattle among most tribes surrounding the Nyanga, and the fact that a few Nyanga chiefs were said to have acquired cattle
in the 1950's (cattle pastured by members of other tribes in the savanna highlands bordering the Nyanga forests). It is also possible that this part of the text may have pre-
served a tradition known by the ancestors of the Nyanga before they migrated from the
East African grasslands into the Congo rain forest. *Batwá/Pygmies*: there are a few small
groups in Nyanga country called Pygmies by the Nyanga which call themselves
Baremba. Physically, they are a mixed breed, visibly strong in Pygmy influences; culturally, their pattern of life is very close to that of the Pygmy. Such Pygmy groups are
affiliated with certain Nyanga chiefs as their hunters and gatherers; they have highly
important ritual duties in connection with the enthronement of chiefs; they have many
privileges, including the permission to harvest freely certain species of bananas,
bandírabitambo/the royal initiators: in each Nyanga state there are from four to seven
officeholders who collectively are called *bandírabitambo* and who exercise important

with seven entrances. When the people were resuscitated, Iyangura began to speak in the middle of the crowd of people, saying: "You, Shemwindo, my brother, in the middle of the whole country of yours, have them prepare much beer and cows and goats; let all the people meet here in Tubondo. It is then that we shall be able to examine in detail all the palavers and to redress them in the assembly." After Shemwindo had heard the voice of his sister Iyangura, he uttered a cry, high and low, to all his people, saying that they should bring beer together.[227] After one week had passed, all groups within his state swarmed into Tubondo, together with beer and meats. On the morning of the eighth day, all the people of all the villages of Shemwindo's state pressed together in the assembly. After all the people, the children and the youngsters, the adults and the elders, had thronged about, Mwindo dressed himself and became like the anus of a snail. His aunt Iyangura, she too threw on her clothes, those famous ones of Mukiti's. His father Shemwindo, he too dressed himself from top to bottom: *tuhuhuma*-bark cloths on which (were) red color and castor oil, *ndorera*-fringes, *masia*-hair ornaments.[228] He too became something beautiful. After the people had grouped themselves in the assembly, servants stretched mats out on the ground, there where Mwindo and his father and his

---

ritual duties in regard to the institution of chieftaincy. *Sábe tu kásángá búri to/again they [the descent groups] became as they were before*: interesting construction which literally could be translated as: they (the descent groups) began to be (*sábe*) again (*to*) habitually in the past (*kásángá*) as are they (the descent groups [*búrito*]). The grammatically correct form for *búrito* is *búriso, -so* bearing on *ésángandá*; but the former euphemistic considerations are in operation here: *-so* is a "dangerous" form because it could mean "your father," and this term must never be used in an ambiguous context, or it might bear on such words as *santsa* (pubic hair) or *nyo/sanyo* (vulva), which must be avoided in normal speech.

227. *rákíra/have them prepare*: lit., to invite people to do some kind of work on one's behalf. *He uttered a cry, high and low*: i.e, he made the best possible appeal; he did his best to call together as many people as possible.

228. *Cébjndj munáná múmukoma-kómá/on the morning of the eighth day*: lit., (the day) of eight days, in the morning, *sakwá Múkiti ésáncangi/her clothes, those famous ones of Mukiti*: lit., of at Mukiti's *the* clothes; our translation "those famous ones" is justified both by the reversal of the normal word order and by the augment. Reference is either to the beautiful clothes she wore when she was married to Mukiti or to clothes she had received from him. *wámbare ákwantsí nëkwjyo/he dressed himself from top to bottom*: interesting use of the current words for land/soil/ below/on the ground (*kwantsí*) and for sky/air/above (*kwiyo*). The expression means that he dressed himself incredibly well.

aunt would pass. All the people in that assembly kept silent pi! There
was sacred silence.[229] Those three radiant stars, Mwindo and his father
and his aunt, appeared from inside the house. They went into the open
to the assembly; they marched solemnly. Those who were in the gathering of the assembly gave them the gift of their eyes: there where they
appeared, that is where their attention was focused. Some among them
surmised, saying: "I wonder, is Shemwindo born with another young
man?" Some answered: "Shemwindo is there with the chief of Shekwa-
bahinga, together with his wife." Some said: "No, Shemwindo is there
with his sister, Mukiti's wife, and (with) Mukiti himself." The remainder
said that Shemwindo was with his sister Iyangura, Mukiti's wife,
together with his son Mwindo, the Little-one-just-born-he-walked, the
man of many wonders, the one who was formerly martyrized by his
father." Shemwindo and Mwindo and Iyangura went in a line, while
appearing in the middle of the gathering of the assembly. Mwindo
beseeched his friend Nkuba, asking him for three copper chairs. Nkuba
made them come down. When they were close to the ground, being
close to the ground, they remained suspended in the air about five
meters from the ground.[230] Mwindo and his father and his aunt climbed
up onto the chairs; Iyangura sat down in the middle of both, Shemwindo
on the right side and Mwindo on the left side. When all the men had
finished grouping themselves together in the assembly and had finished becoming silent, Mwindo stood up from his chair; he raised his
eyes into the air, he implored Nkuba, saying: "Oh, my friend Nkuba,
prevent the sky from falling!"[231] Having spoken like that, he lowered his
eyes toward the ground, down upon the mass of people; he said, he
lauded them, saying: "Be strong, you chiefs." They approved of it. He
said: "You counselors, be strong." They approved of it. Then he: "You
seniors, be strong." They approved. Mwindo praised the council, holding all the things with which he was born: *conga*, axe, the little bag in

229. *pįl*: onomatopoeia to stress the completeness of the silence.

230. *métero/meters*: Nyangaized French word *mètre*.

231. *uhángenga ébųtų/prevent the sky from falling*: the verb *ihánge* means to protect
something from falling by supporting it (e.g., said about banana trees with many heavy
stems, which have to be propped with gaffs). Mwindo may be implying two things: first,
he seems to ask the divinity of lightning to prevent rain from falling; second, he seems
to boast about his weight (importance) and that of his aunt and his father who are also
sitting in copper chairs suspended from the sky.

which the rope was; he also held an ancient stick to praise the council.[232] After Mwindo had finished praising those who were in the council, he made a proclamation: "Among the seven groups that are here in
Tubondo, may each group be seated together in a cluster; and the chiefs
and the seniors of the other villages, may they also be seated in their
(own) cluster." After he had finished speaking like that, the people
grouped themselves in an orderly manner, each group in its own cluster. Mwindo also ordered that all his seven mothers be seated in one
group but that Nyamwindo, the mother who gave birth to him, should
separate herself somewhat from his little mothers. After he had spoken
like that, his mothers moved (to form) their own cluster; his mother
who gave birth to him moved a short distance away (yet remaining)
near her co-spouses. Mwindo also ordered: "Now you, my father, it is
your turn. Explain to the chiefs the reason why you have had a grudge
against me; if I have taken a portion larger than yours, if I have borne
ill will against you because of your goods, if I have snatched them away
from you, tell the chiefs the news so that they may understand." Where
Shemwindo was sitting, he was flabbergasted: sweat arose from his big
toe, climbed up to his testicles, went to arrive at the hair on his head; in
his virile impetus Shemwindo got up. Because of the great shame in the
eyes of Shemwindo, he did not even praise the chiefs anymore; he
spoke while quivering, and a little spitting cough clung to the centipede
of his throat, without warning: (all this) caused by the great evil of
destruction.[233]

232. This passage is typical of the way in which a solemn meeting among the
Nyanga begins. The main speaker recites a number of formulas wishing strength and
long life to all participants; he then asks for the blessing of specific categories of persons.
All participants answer in chorus aé (yes), translated here as "they approved." The praise
formula used by Mwindo, músaruké (be strong), is unusual, the more common formula
being karamo (force, life, good health) or músinjé (be praised). The verbal form isaruka
seems to be a reversive of isara (to vomit), i.e., may you not vomit (may you be cold),
nkóma yĕkibúyá/an ancient stick: kibúyá is an uncommon word that might be derived
from Babúya, a descent group to which the narrator was related. Members of the
descent group were said to have been the first to make the Mwindo epic known. If this
interpretation is correct, the narrator would mean that the stick Mwindo was holding
was one of the sacred emblems of the Babúya group.

233. The shame and hesitation of Shemwindo is powerfully described in this passage; in no other Nyanga text can a depiction so richly evocative of emotions and physical reactions be found.

Shemwindo said:

All you chiefs who are here, I don't deny all the evil that I have
done against this, my offspring, my son; indeed, I had passed an
interdiction on my wives in the middle of the group of counselors and nobles, stating that I would kill the one among my
wives who would give birth to a son, together with her child.
Among all the wives, six among them gave birth only to girls,
and it was my beloved-one who gave birth to a boy. After my
beloved-one had given birth to a boy, I despised her; my preferred wife became my despised-one. From then on, I always
looked at the soles of her feet. In the middle of all this anger, I
armed myself with a spear; I threw it into the birth hut six times;
I wanted to kill the child with its mother. When I saw that the
child was not dead, I made an agreement with the counselors
and the nobles; they threw this child away into a grave. When
we woke up in the morning, upon awakening, we saw the child
already wailing again in its mother's house. When I noticed that,
I asked myself in my heart, I said: "If I continue to fail to kill this
child, then it will oust me from my royal chair; now I, here, have
seen all these amazing things that he is doing, so this child will
cause me a big problem." It's only then that I carried him into the
drum and that I threw him into the river. Where this child went,
I believed that I was harming him, whereas I was only making
him strong(er). From there it is that this child's anger stems.
When he came out of the river he marched right up against me;
he attacked me here in Tubondo; it is from that point on that I
began to flee, all my people having been exterminated. Where I
fled, I rejoiced, saying, "I was safe," (thinking) that where I was
going, there was salvation, whereas I was casting myself into the
thorns of rambling around throughout the country counting
tree roots, sleeping in a filthy place, eating bad foods.[234] From
that moment on, my son set out in search of me; he went to take
me away in the abyss of evil in which I was involved; he went to
seize me at the country's border. I was at that time withered like

234. In an unusually florid style, Shemwindo gives an admirable summary of the
main events of the conflict with his son.

dried bananas. And it is like that that I arrive here in the village of Tubondo. So may the male progeny be saved, because it has let me see the way in which the sky becomes daylight and has (given me) the joy of witnessing again the warmth of the people and of all the things [of] here in Tubondo.

Iyangura spoke to the men who were sitting in the assembly, reproaching openly their young man here, Shemwindo:[235]

Here I am, aunt of Mwindo, you chiefs, in your presence. Our young man here, Shemwindo, has married me out to Mukiti; I got accustomed to it (thanks to) the confidence of my husband.[236] Thanks to my labor and to getting along with him, my husband placed me high up, so that he loved me above all the wives he had married. So then—you chiefs, may I not bore you; let me not carry you far off in a long line of many words. Suddenly, this child appeared where I lived; Mukiti was then on the verge of killing him because he did not know that he was my child; but his intelligence and his malice saved him.[237] It is from then on that I followed him and followed him to point out to him the way to Shemwindo's, and (also because of my) desire to see him. It's there that Mwindo's fights with his father began, because of the anger (caused by) all the evils that his father perpetrated against him. He subdued this village, Tubondo; his father fled. Where he fled, Mwindo went in search of him, saying that his father should not go to die in the leaves.[238] When he joined him, he seized him; it is that, that Mwindo has made his

---

235. *Shemwindo*: the narrator mistakenly said that Iyangura reproached Mwindo. The context indicates that she is critical of Shemwindo and not of Mwindo. *musike wăbó/their young man*: a term used by women to refer to their brothers.

236. *bănu murĵkĵre/in your presence*: lit., you are seated, *iwé wámenyera na ko/I got accustomed to it*: the verb *ĵmenyera* is used for women who become well adapted to their husband's family and village and do not find excuses for frequently visiting their own families. *n'erĵrĵsĵenyu* in the next sentence, translated as "getting along," literally means to make each other say yes.

237. In contrast to Shemwindo, Iyangura is talkative; she cannot easily or adequately summarize a situation.

238. *die in the leaves*: i.e., die like an animal rambling around in the forest.

father return again to this village, Tubondo. So it is that we are in this meeting of the assembly of the chiefs.

She also said:

You, Shemwindo, acted badly, together with your counselors and nobles. If it were a counselor from whom this plan of torment against Mwindo had emanated, then his throat would be cut, here in the council. But you are safe, it being yourself from whom this plan sprang. You have acted badly, you Shemwindo, when you discriminated against the children, saying that some were bad and others good, whereas you did not know what was in the womb of your wife; what you were given by Ongo, you saw it to be bad; the good (thing) turned into the bad one. So, there is nothing good on earth! But nevertheless, we are satisfied, you notables, (because of) the way in which we are up on our feet again here in Tubondo, but this Shemwindo has committed an iniquitous deed. If the people had been exterminated here, it is Shemwindo who would have been guilty of exterminating them. I, Iyangura, I finish, I am at this point.[239]

After Iyangura had finished speaking, Mwindo also stood up; he praised the assembly, he said:

As for me, I, Mwindo, man of many feats, the Little-one-just-born-he-walked, I am not holding a grudge against my father; may my father here not be frightened, believing that I am still angry with him; no, I am not angry with my father. What my father did against me and what I did against my father, all that is already over. Now let us examine what is to come, the evil and the good; the one of us who will again start beginning, it is he who will be in the wrong, and all those seniors here will be the witnesses of it. Now, let us live in harmony in our country, let us care for our people well.

Shemwindo declared that as far as he was concerned, the act of giving birth was not repugnant in itself. (He said that) where he was here,

---

239. *Ongo*: name for the creator god. *nendĕ mpe/I am at this point*: lit., I go, I arrive until here (in my story), the formula regularly used to finish a speech.

no longer was he chief, that now it was Mwindo who remained in his succession, that against the one who would insult Mwindo in this land the seniors would clap their hands.[240] When Mwindo heard his father's voice, he answered him: "You, father, just sit down on your royal chair; I cannot be chief as long as you are alive, (otherwise) I would die suddenly. Where the counselors and nobles were seated, they assented to Mwindo; they said to Shemwindo: "Your son did not speak wrongly; divide the country into two parts; let your son take a part and you a part, since, if you were to give away all authority, you would again be immensely jealous of him, and this jealously could eventually trouble this country in the long run." Shemwindo said: "No, you counselors and nobles, I am not on that side; but I want my son to become chief. From now on I shall always work behind him." The counselors told him: "You, Shemwindo, divide your country into two parts, you a part and your son a part, since formerly you always used to say that you alone were a man surpassing (all) others; and what you said happened: that is why we witnessed all these palavers; we had no way of disagreeing with you because you inspired fear. Lo! if the chief cannot be disagreed with, then it is too great foolishness." Shemwindo said: "Since you, my counselors and my nobles, come to give this advice, so I am ready to divide the country into two parts: Mwindo a part and I, Shemwindo, a part, because of the fear (you inspire); but in my own name I had wanted to leave the country to Mwindo, and from then on I would always have been eating food after my son Mwindo, because I have felt and do feel much shame in the face of my son and of all the people.[241]

After Shemwindo had spoken like that, he conferred the kingship upon his son: he stripped himself of all the things of kingship which he bore: a dress dyed red and two red belts; he also gave him *butea watukushi* to wear on his arms when he would pile up the *bsebse*-meat, and *butea* (to wear) on the legs; he also gave him a *ncambi*-belt; he also

240. *the seniors would clap their hands*: as a denunciation of him. *jkón-góta* literally refers to the gestures made to remove dust from something.

241. The Nyanga text accounts for a common habit of splitting existing states into two or more smaller autonomous ones. Currently the sub-diving is never between a ruling chief and his son; at the death of a chief, however, the state may be divided between two or more of his sons by different ritual wives.

gave him a *kataba*-belt; he also gave him a *kembo*-hat; he also gave him the hide of a white goat.[242] Shemwindo dressed Mwindo (in) all those things while Mwindo was standing up, because a chief is always being dressed in (such) things while standing. The counselors went to fetch the chair imbued with *ukaru*-powder and castor oil; they gave it to Shemwindo; Shemwindo made Mwindo sit on it. Shemwindo handed over to Mwindo the scepter of copper on which there were lamels imbued with *ukaru*-powder and castor oil. He (Shemwindo) handed these things over to him when he was already seated on the chair. When he stood up, his father also handed over to him the wrist protector and the bow; he also gave him the quiver in which there were arrows.[243] Shemwindo also handed Pygmies over to his son; he gave him the *bandirabitambo*-initiators: *mwamihesi, mushonga, mubei, mushumbiya, muheri, shemumbo*, counselors, nobles.[244] They dressed him (in) all these things in the guesthouse. After Shemwindo had enthroned his son like that, Mwindo shouted that he now had become famous, that he would not want (to act) as his father had so that only one descent group would remain on earth. "May all the descent groups establish themselves in the country; may boys and girls be born; may there be born deaf and cripples, because a country is never without

242. Enumeration of various items of traditional paraphernalia of chiefs: the dress is made of bark cloth dyed red with a mixture of castor oil and camwood powder; the bells are of raphia dyed red; *butea watukushi* are little rings made of string obtained from the raphia palm and are used as money as well as for ornaments; *tukushi* signifies that the rings are worn as armlets; *bsebse*-meat is a strange word, the exact meaning of which I could not obtain; *ncambi*-belt is made of wild boar skin and decorated with leopard, monkey, and genet teeth; *kataba*-belt is made of raphia and is decorated with beads, cowries, and wild boar's hair; *kembo*-hat is made of the skins of genet, flying squirrel, and bush baby.

243. The chair and the ceremonial spear are some of the royal emblems, as are the wrist protector, the bow, the quiver, and the arrows. The wrist protector is made of the skin of a bush baby and filled with moss and other ingredients; the quiver is made of bark stained black; the arrows have no iron heads and are poisoned.

244. A Nyanga chief is supposed to have some Pygmies (physically miscegenated, but culturally close to Pygmies) to hunt and to perform important ritual duties for him. He also has a number of ritual experts whose titles are mentioned: *mwamihesi*, the chief blacksmith; *mushonga*, the cook; *mubei*, the barber; *mushumbiya*, the drummer; *muheri*, the sacrificer. A chief also has his advisors (*bakungú*), nobles (*barúsi*). Among these nobles there is a *she-mumbo*, one who provides the chief with the ritual wife whose son will succeed to the throne.

(some) handicapped-ones."[245] After Shemwindo had dressed his son in the chiefly paraphernalia, he distributed beer and meat for the chiefs who were there; each group took a goat and a cow. They also gave Iyangura one cow for returning to her husband Mukiti. The chiefs and the counselors who were there said: "Let Mwindo remain here in Tubondo and let Shemwindo go to dwell on another mountain." Hearing this, Shemwindo clapped his hands; he was very satisfied. During Mwindo's enthonement, his uncles, the Baniyana, gave him a maiden, and Shamwami also gave him a maiden; Mwindo's father, he too, gave him a maiden called Katobororo and the Pygmies gave him one.[246] During Mwindo's enthronement, he was given only four women; he went on getting himself married while he was crossing the country. In each place where he made a blood pact he carried off a maiden.[247] During Mwindo's enthronement, the convives grew weary; some of them defecated on (their) heels. After Mwindo had been enthroned, the assembly dispersed: all those who came from somewhere returned there; Shemwindo also took possession of his mountain; he left to his son Tubondo.[248] When Iyangura, aunt of Mwindo, returned to her husband, she annointed Mwindo in the middle of the group saying:

245. *wamasíma/he now had become famous*: the verb *isíma* designates the status and power one achieves through initiation into an association or through enthronement rites.

246. At the chief's enthronement, as suggested in this passage, there are two basic types of exchanges taking place. The chief gives the participants food to be consumed during the ceremonies and other valuables (e.g., goats) to take home; he also assigns portions of land to the incumbents of the ritual offices mentioned in n. 244. On the other hand, the chief receives, without matrimonial payments, wives from several categories of people: one from a very close agnatic relative (his father or brother), one from the Pygmies, one from his maternal uncles, one from *Shé-* (or *shá*) *mwǎmí* (lit., the father of the chief) who is in charge of the protection of the chief's ritual wife.

247. A Nyanga marriage is often preceded by a contract of blood brotherhood between the groom and his wife's brother or between the groom's father and the father of the bride.

248. *mutundu/mountain*: the Nyanga possess two generic terms for mountain, *ntata*, a "father mountain," and *mutundu*, a "child mountain." The meaning of this distinction is that in the legal and political sphere, persons in control of a *mutundu* are subordinate to those ruling a *ntata*, because *mutundu* is considered to be a mountain or, better, a unit of land resulting from a partition of *ntata*. This passage implies that Shemwindo is considered to be politically less powerful than his son Mwindo.

Oh, Mwindo, hail!
Blessing, here, hail!
If your father throws you into the grave, hail!
Don't harbor resentment, hail!
May you stand up and make your first step, hail!
May you be safe, may you be blessed, hail!
And your father and your mother, hail!
May you bring forth tall children, boys and girls.
Be strong, my father; as for me, there is nothing ominous
    left, hail![249]

When Mwindo took leave of his father, his father also gave him a blessing. Mwindo handed over to his aunt two counselors to accompany her; he also gave her four goats and a return gift of twenty baskets of rice and five little chicken baskets.

After a fixed number of days had elapsed since he had been enthroned, Mwindo said that he had a terrible craving to eat some wild pig meat. He sent his Pygmies out to hunt (for it) in the forest. Where the Pygmies went in the forest, when they were already "in the place of coming whence, going where," they felt tired, they slept half way.[250] In the morning they set out right after awakening. In leaving right after awakening, they found the trail of wild pigs; they followed them; in going say "from here to there," they met them; they sent the dogs after them, seeing that they were fleeing; the dogs hurled themselves after them.[251] Crossing two plateaus, they met a red-haired pig

---

249. Blessings (anointment of the chest, accompanied by supplicatory prayers) are extremely frequent among the Nyanga, particularly among kinsmen, on a variety of social occasions. *úsingiriré/May you stand up and make your first step*: the verb *isingirira* means the first efforts of walking made by a baby; the meaning here is: may you be successful, may you be in good health. *May you bring forth tall children*: i.e., of the best stature according to the Nyanga norms.

250. *mûntúka-kúnį na mwienda-kúnį/in the place of coming whence, going where*: in this currently used expression, the Nyanga do not think in terms of place, but of a state of mind. The entire phrase could be rendered as follows: when they were in the state of wandering whence to come and where to go. The expression is used to indicate a great distance traveled.

251. *they sent the dogs*: the Nyanga hold the hunting dogs on leash until they have tracked down the hunted animals, *bana-mbíbi bírása/the dogs hurled themselves*: the verb *írása* literally stands for the action of shooting an arrow.

dragging its scrotum; they hurled a sharp spear at it. The pig in question said that it was not great—it turned its hoofs upward; it died.[252] They cut it into pieces on the spot. There where they were in the very dense forest, when they were cutting the pig to pieces, Dragon heard their mumbling.[253] Dragon said: "What now, people here again? I always thought that I was the only one living here, whereas there are still other people there." Dragon went after them, snakelike. When he came close to them, he threw himself onto them; he took away three Pygmies from there; he swallowed them. One among the Pygmies was called Nkurongo; he wrestled himself loose; he fled, and the dogs followed him; they fled with him. Dragon said to himself: "Let this wild pork remain here, for I will trap the dogs and the Pygmy, the one who fled. Dragon nestled down beside the corpse of the pig. Where Nkurongo fled, when he arrived, say "over there," he looked back saying: "Lo! our companions have been overtaken by night; they are already dead." At the time when he fixed his eyes on him (the Dragon), he saw that he had seven heads and seven horns and seven eyes. He said: "This time it is an enormous lump; Mwindo, who is usually capable against people, this time will be powerless against this one in fighting with him."[254] When that little Pygmy there was already on the crest, he shouted: "I flee, eh!" He kicked up his heels onto his shoulders; he fled and the dogs followed him. He went to appear in the village of Tubondo; when he was nearly bursting with breath, he arrived in Mwindo's house. After he had rested awhile, "for as long as it takes

252. *dragging its scrotum*: i.e., an old, fat pig. *Muna-katuku/the pig in question*: the form *muna-*, which generally indicates the species or group, here seems to have the rare meaning of "in question." *The pig in question said that it was not great*: i.e., the pig had not the force to resist. *ÿákwa/it died*: it is as if the pig died as the result of its own decision.

253. *Kirímu/Dragon*: Kirimu frequently occurs in Nyanga tales. He is described as a big animal with black hide, seven heads, teeth like a dog, huge belly, and tail of an eagle. The monster lives on the ground in dense forest and is a solitary hunter that occasionally feeds on human beings. In some tales Kirimu is said to have a human wife whom he captured. The precise details of the seizure are not given. He never has children of his own, but occasionally he keeps a human child whom he treats well, fattening him in order to eat him later. In the Nyanga tales Kirimu is regularly killed by a clever man, a hero, or even by a young child who destroys him with a knife after letting himself be swallowed or who kills him by throwing hot stones into his mouth or by cutting a rope by which he is trying to climb a tree.

254. *butúmámba/ enormous lump*: lit., a heap of soil, a dike.

a pot of paste to be cooked," Mwindo asked him: "Peace there, from where you are coming?" He answered him: "There is no peace there, you [my] chief! We went to the forest, four of us; Dragon has swallowed three (of us), and I, Nkurongo, escaped among them, together with the dogs. But it is not Dragon; he is as large as the sky." Hearing that, Mwindo said: "Well, now, this time it's tough; my Pygmies in their very first hunt are already exterminated in the forest." He looked up to the sky, lowered his eyes to the ground; he said: "Oh, my *conga*, be victorious in the day of tomorrow." And that day his father, Shemwindo, was in the village. Mwindo said to his father: "The rooster is going to die of *mukerį*, I shall already be on my way; I shall go right after awakening with this Pygmy only to fight with Dragon."[255] When Shemwindo heard this, he forbade his son: "Oh, my father, no, don't go there; Dragon has always been a destroyer; he has eaten from man's bones; if you again provoke this Dragon, then you cause great (disaster) in this country."[256] Mwindo said to his father: "I do not care, at any rate, I am going from dawn on; you stay behind to tell the counselors that I have gone to fight with Dragon."

When it was very early morning, Mwindo took up his *conga*, and the Pygmy preceded him. They thus proceeded in the forest. When they appeared at the place where they had cut the pig into pieces, the Pygmy pointed at Dragon, saying: "There he is." Mwindo said to the Pygmy: "Stop first; let me take a look at him." Mwindo said to the Pygmy: "You, stay here. When Dragon will have swallowed me, it is you who will announce the news in the village." Mwindo took his subduer of a *conga*; he went snakelike after the Dragon. When he saw himself eye-to-eye with him, Mwindo designated him, saying: "You will not judge me; today: you and I." Dragon was seized with surprise; he stood up. When he was about to fly against Mwindo, Mwindo put sweet words into his mouth, he sang:

255. *The rooster is going to die of mukerį*: Mwindo means to say that he will be on his way long before the rooster crows. The Nyanga hate the matutinal crowing of the rooster; they find it ominous and fear it to be an announcement of death in the village. People curse the rooster by saying "may you die of mukerį"; mukerį is the name of a disease, but it is also used as a synonym for malediction.

256. *cámarángá mukakụa ná kakụa kábea/he has eaten from man's bones*: lit., he has been eating (since long ago and continues to do so) from the bone and bone of men (from many a man's bones).

Dragon, you are helpless against Mwindo,
For Mwindo is the Little-one-just-born-he-walked.
Dragon, you have challenged Mwindo.
Dragon, you are powerless against Mwindo,
For Mwindo is the Little-one-just-born-he-walked.
Shemwindo gave birth to a hero.
Comrade, you are powerless against Mwindo.

When Dragon attempted to swallow Mwindo, Mwindo exclaimed: "This time he is finished." Mwindo also approached where he was; Mwindo beat him (with) his *conga*. Dragon fell upside down; he died. Mwindo called, shouting to his Pygmy to come to cut up the Dragon. The Pygmy came. When he was about to touch the Dragon with his great knife, Mwindo forbade him, saying: "First, leave him like that; let us call people in the village so that they may go and carry him to the village in order that Shemwindo could see the wonders that I perform." Mwindo implored those who were in the village; Mwindo sent his *conga* to the village to go and bring the people so that they could go and fetch this god of a dragon. He sang:

Oh, my *conga,* go for me.
Those who have remained in Tubondo over there,
Those who have remained in Tubondo over there,
At Shemwindo's,
May Shemwindo send people to me.

Where *conga* went, when it arrived in Tubondo, it arrived just in front of Shemwindo. It wagged itself in front of him, and all the people of the village abandoned (their homes); they went to see the way in which *conga* was wagging itself before Shemwindo. Shemwindo said that *conga* is giving the news: "If Mwindo is not dead, it is Dragon who is dead." Shemwindo sent there a group of people saying:

Be ready to leave the village![257]
Go and join Mwindo!
In the dense forest there are many (things);

257. *Muna-kįtų/comrade*: the term is usually employed in reference to a kinsman; it occurs in disputes to designate (somewhat pejoratively, like the French *mon cher*) the opponent. The implication is also that Mwindo treats Kirimu not like a superior force, but like a kind of congener. *Múkaí ékwįkúra/be ready to leave the village*: lit., look at the way out of the village; have the eyes fixed at the exit.

There are snakes that bite.
Go and join Mwindo,
Where Mwindo has gone.
Shemwindo has given birth to a hero.

Having wagged itself in front of Shemwindo, the *conga* flew away, together with the people whom Shemwindo had provided. *Conga* was flying with those people through the air; it went to descend with the people at the place where Mwindo was. When Mwindo saw his *conga* with the people, *conga* came into Mwindo's hands. Mwindo said to the men to lift up Dragon. They made a stretcher; they put Dragon on top of (it). Some among them seized the pig that had been killed by the Pygmy. When the carriers of Dragon had left say "as far as that," the stretcher broke because of Dragon's weight. They made another stretcher; they put Dragon on it again; they lifted him up; they had him arrive at the village. When he (Dragon) appeared in the village, the whole village crowded together: so many young, so many old people![258] They let Dragon down in the middle of the village. When the people saw him, they were very astonished; they whooped, they said: "Now, things will be coming out of the forest!" Some among them said: "At any rate, he who has killed this one cannot fail to kill one of his relatives." When Mwindo heard those people speaking like that, he killed them on the spot; they were three; they died.[259] Mwindo said to his people to cut up Dragon, and he, Mwindo, sang.

Dragon is being skinned and cut up on the little raphia palms.[260]
Shemwindo howled, saying:
Dragon is being skinned and cut up on the little raphia palms.
Dragon always devours people;
Dragon has exterminated people.
Shemwindo, my father, be afraid of me.

258. *nébanụnké, nébanụnké, nébakúngú nèbakúngú/so many young! so many old people!*: astonishment about their number is expressed here through word repetition, an appropriate gesture, and through the insistence on final vowels.

259. *bátúra ésândụrụ/they whooped*: this expression renders the action of producing whoops by beating the palm of the hand against the open mouth, shouting *uuu*. It is viewed as a manifestation of enthusiasm and astonishment. *wácịnja/he killed*: Nyangaized Swahili verb *kucinja* (to kill). The Nyanga form is *wákera*.

260. *híyótubondo/on the little raphia palms*: a pun, because Dragon is being skinned in the village of Tubondo and is spread out on raphia leaves (*tubondo*).

When they opened the belly, there came out a man who leaped up, being alive; there came out another man; he came out; he too was alive. When they opened the belly, there came out another one who leaped up, being alive. After Dragon had been cut up and the three Pygmies had come out alive, Mwindo gave the order that he personally wanted (the following): "When you will begin to eat this Dragon, you will eat him with bones and all; don't throw any of them away." After Dragon had been cut up, Mwindo distributed to all his people all the meat with the mass of bones; he told them also that in case he would see a little bone behind somebody's house, he would make him pay for (it). When Dragon had been divided up and divided again into many parts, they seized his eyes; they roasted them hot on a piece of potsherd. Each time that there appeared a splatter and it burst open, there came out a man. When all the eyes of Dragon had been roasted, there appeared one thousand people. Mwindo said: "These are my people." And he gave them a mountain.[261]

Where Nkuba resided in the sky it so happened that he had made a blood pact with Dragon. Where Nkuba was in the sky, when he inhaled the odor of his friend Dragon, which was passing with the wind, froth dropped from his nose; tears came out his eyes; he said: "What shall I do with this friend here, Mwindo?" He said that he first wanted to make him suffer in order that he would not begin again. "When I shall have finished making him suffer here where I am, then I shall know to return him to earth to his village." He also said: "If Mwindo had known that he had exchanged blood with Dragon, then he would not have killed his friend the Dragon; in that case, he would not restore him; in that case, he would be lost right here, without having gone back to his country. But he is safe because he did not know that he was my friend."

Mwindo sang:

Nkuba has just come to take Mwindo;
Nkuba came to carry Mwindo away

261. *báhụmo/they opened (the belly): ịhúmo* literally means to remove a dike (stone in some types of fishing) or to make a hole in a pot (so as to take out something), *he gave them a mountain*: it is customary for a Nyanga chief to bestow upon individuals and groups that place themselves under his protection a title of perpetual usufruct over parts of his domain.

From the heights of Tubondo,
When he inhaled the smell (of roasting).
Mwindo howled, he said:
Eh! Nkuba, you are helpless against Mwindo;
Shemwindo brought forth a hero.
Eh! Nkuba, you are helpless against Mwindo Mboru.

Mwindo said:

Eh! Nkuba, you are helpless against Mwindo Mboru.
The cheerleaders were always in unison.
The tunes that are being sung, the noninitiates cannot understand
them.
Oh, scribe, you,
You see that I am already going;
My mother who carried me,
You see that I am already going.
The counselors of Shemwindo,
You see that I am already going.
Let the counselors of Shemwindo come here.
Kubikubi-star adheres to moon.
My friend Nkuba, be victorious.
Nkuba has come to take Mwindo.
Let us climb up to Nyaṛṛe's.

Mwindo said farewell (to the people), one by one.

My mother who carried me,
You are seeing that I am already going.
Nyamwindo howled, complaining.
—And Nkuba at that very moment had just opened (the door)—
"What shall I do with my child?"
Nyamwindo howled, saying:
"I die, I die, along with my child."
Shemwindo howled, saying:
"I die, I die, along with my child."
The little bark loincloth that the Bira debarked,
If it gets used, I set aside the trimming.[262]

262. This song combines four things: first, Mwindo himself predicts and describes the coming of Nkuba; second, Mwindo predicts his own salvation; third, the narrator inserts some of his own proverbial reflections; finally, the narrator describes some of the

After Nkuba had inhaled the smell of his friend Dragon which came from his friend Mwindo in Tubondo, he descended on the spot to take Mwindo. He descended; he arrived in Mwindo's village. Nkuba said to Mwindo: "I come to take you, you my friend; I want to go and teach you because I am very vexed with you, you my friend, since you dared to kill Dragon, whereas Dragon was my friend; so know that you are doing wrong." Hearing this, Mwindo was not afraid of going away with his friend; but his people were stricken with anxiety, thinking that their chief was going forever. Mwindo sang:

> Let us go up to Bisherya over there,
> For Nkuba has come to take Mwindo.
> I am about to climb up to Bisherya over there,
> For Nkuba has come to take Mwindo.
> Oh, Nkuba, you are powerless against Mwindo,
> For Mwindo is the Little-one-just-born-he-has-walked.
> Shemwindo gave birth to a hero;
> My friend, you are powerless against Mwindo.
> Wanderer, go anyway announcing it,
> That *ntiriri*-liana has become *mubanga*-rope,
> And *musara*-liana. has become *mukendo*-bag.[263]
> What Shemwindo has said
> Will be lacking the one who will analyze it.
> The sky became day while we were still talking,
> Like the association-*mukuki*.[264]

action pertinent to the departure of Mwindo: the arrival of Nkuba ("And Nkuba at that very moment had just opened the door), the complaints of Mwindo's father and mother. *nabíka murando/I set aside the trimming*: i.e., I keep part of it as a souvenir.

263. *Bisherya*: used as a synonym for sky, but it is also one of the places frequently mentioned in the accounts of the early migration of the Nyanga from East Africa. *The ntiriri-liana . . .*: proverb complaining about the reversal of the normal order of things: the *mubanga* carrying-rope is not normally made from lianas, but from raphia, and so is the *mukendo* shoulder bag.

264. *Búrí nkandá mukúkj/like the association mukuki*: The main initiatory object of this association is a sound box (through which the spirit of the association manifests itself); *nkandá* literally means a package (in which the sound box is wrapped). The narrator says that throughout the night they spoke about mysterious things, like the ones revealed by the sound box in the *mukuki* initiations.

The-ones-who-are-accustomed-to-go-to-sleep, let them go
    to sleep.
May the one who is always grumbling remain grumbling.
The counselors of Shemwindo,
The counselors threw me into troubles.
Let me speak to Munguto of Wamba,
Where there are chiefs' wives carrying raphia bunches.
I have spoken with my companion odiously;
In case the heart turns away from where it has come: it
    means it is getting accustomed.[265]
Kabarebare and Ntabare,
My father,
Where the husband of my senior sister sets up *byoo*-traps.

Mwindo went on singing like that while Nkuba was climbing up
slowly with him into the air, and the people of Mwindo had their attention diverted by (what was happening) above. Nkuba disappeared into
the clouds, together with Mwindo; and they arrived at Nkuba's. When
Mwindo arrived at Nkuba's, Nkuba asked him: "You, my friend Mwindo,
you have acted badly when you dared to kill my friend Dragon, when
you have roasted his eyes so that the odor climbed up to me, so that I
smelled it in the air; if only you had made the odor descend to earth,
then I would not have been angry." Nkuba still said to Mwindo: "I have
rescued you many times from many dangers, so then you show that you
are equal to me." Mwindo arrived there at Nkuba's; he felt there much
cold, and the icy wind there was strong. No house! They lived there in
mere nomadism, no settling in one spot. Nkuba seized Mwindo; he
climbed up with him to Rain. When Rain saw Mwindo, he told him:
"You, Mwindo, never accept being criticized; the news about your
toughness, your heroism, we surely have heard the news, but over here,
there is no room for your heroism." Rain fell upon Mwindo seven and
seven times more; he had Hail fall upon him, and he soaked him thor-
oughly. Mwindo said: "This time I am in trouble in every way." Nkuba

---

265. *kátima/odiously*: lit., little heart. *Kútuké mutíma nti ịbera/In case the heart
turns away from where it has come: it means it is getting accustomed*: free translation that
tries to capture the spirit of this very succinct Nyanga dictum; lit., that the heart leaves
a place it is to get used. When one forgets his place of origin, it is a sign of being well
accustomed to the new place of residence (said about married women).

lifted Mwindo up again; he had him ramble across Moon's domain. When Moon saw Mwindo, he pointed at him: "This time the news was given us that you were tough, but here in the sky there is no room for your pride." Moon burned Mwindo's hair; Mwindo complained: "Oh, father Shemwindo, bless me, and may my *conga* not get out of my hands." Nkuba lifted Mwindo up again; he went and climbed up with him to the domain of Sun. When Sun saw Mwindo, he harassed him hotly; Mwindo lacked all means (of defense) against Sun; his throat became dry; thirst strangulated him; he asked for water. They said to him: "No, there is never any water; now we advise you to grit your teeth; we advise you to put your heart on your knee." After Sun had made Mwindo sustain these pains, Nkuba lifted Mwindo up; he went and made him arrive in the domain of Star. When Star saw him, he pointed him out; he told him: "The news about you was given us that surely you are very tough, but here there is no room for your heroism." *Kubikubi*-star ordered Rain and Sun (to come). All—Nkuba, Rain, Sun, Star—all those told Mwindo but one single thing: "We have respect for you, just that much; otherwise, you would vanish right here. You, Mwindo, you are ordered to go back; never a day should you kill an animal of the forest or of the village or even an insect like a centipede or like a *ntsine*. If one day we would learn the news that you began again to kill a thing among those that we just forbade, then you will die, then your people would never see you again." They pulled his ears seven times and seven more, saying: "Understand?" And he: "Yes, I have understood."[266] They

---

266. This powerful passage relating Mwindo's sufferings in the realm of Lightning, Rain, Moon, Sun, and Star contains a number of evocative expressions that necessitated a free translation, e.g., *rain fell upon Mwindo*: the verb *ihíta* (to descend a mountain) suggests the violence of the falling rain; *he had hail fall upon him*: the verb *isuruca* (to knock over a banana tree or to knock a stem down from a banana tree) describes the power of the action; *Sun harassed him hotly*: the Nyanga text says Sun stretched him out (like an animal hide set out for drying) on hot, hot things; *thirst strangulated him*: the verb *ikáma* describes the action of kneading bananas for beer-brewing, *we advise you to put your heart on your knee*: this expression is used to describe strong, but contained, suffering. When suffering intensely, the Nyanga, in order to restrain from crying, holds his mouth firmly against the knee or arm as if biting it. *ntsine*: a water strider. *Bámu-kokota ématé/they pulled his ears*: the Nyangaized Swahili verb *kukokota* (to pull) is used here instead of the Nyanga *kurwa*, a gesture certainly inspired by what the narrator himself was able to observe in European milieus, *never a day should you kill an animal . . .*: the prohibition against hunting and trapping holds for all Nyanga chiefs.

also said to Mwindo: "It is Nkuba here who is your guardian; if you have done wrong, it is Nkuba who will give the news, and that day he will seize you all at once, without any longer saying farewell to your people.[267]

After Nkuba had made Mwindo ramble everywhere through the sky, they gave him back (the right) of home, saying he was allowed to return. On his return, Mwindo had then finished spending one year in the sky, seeing all the good and all the bad things that are in the sky. Nkuba raised Mwindo up; he returned with him home to Tubondo. Mwindo threw sweet words into his mouth; he sang:

> Mwindo was already arriving
> Where Shemwindo had remained;
> Where Shemwindo had remained
> Mwindo was already arriving

> He who went away returns.
> Shemwindo brought forth a hero.
> What will die and what will be safe,
> Oh my senior sister, may it join Mwindo!
> My friend Nkuba, be victorious.
> Let me go to Tubondo,
> To Tubondo, village of my mothers.[268]
> May I see my mother.
> I descend here in Tubondo,
> In father's village, my dearest one.
> And if, Mwindo, you kill a game,
> It is I who have a right to the tail,
> In which (normally) father's elder brother has a right.[269]

267. *mucuŋgi/guardian*: Nyangaized Swahili word; the Nyanga word would be *muraŋgi*.

268. *village of my mothers*: Tubondo is, in fact, the village of his father and his father's agnatic kinsmen. It is not astonishing for Mwindo to say that it is the village of his mothers: his own mother and the other wives of his father (who are also called mothers in Nyanga practice) inhabit this village. Mwindo wants to make it clear that Tubondo is the village where his own mother—for whom he has a tender love—resides.

269. *And if, Mwindo, you kill a game/It is I who have a right to the tail/In which (normally) father's elder brother has a right*: the text is difficult because of succinctness and the reversal of word order. The correct interpretation is that Mwindo brings to his people the message that from now on all tails (of buffalo and elephant and wild boar) are to be given to him rather than to his father's elder brother, even though his father's elder brother is his senior by birth.

The will says: "Mwindo, if you kill an animal, then you die."[270]

> Oh Mwindo, never try again!
> From now on may you refuse meat.
> Nkuba said:
> "Never try again."
> Shemwindo, you brought forth a hero.
> Kiruka-Mbura, advise those leaving
> Who makes the trees fall in the forest.[271]
> My little father, my dearest one,
> My little father threw me into palavers.
> Substitute, replace me now![272]
> My father believed that I would faint away;
> He threw me into palavers.
> Iyobora, open for me now,
> Iyobora of Mirabyo.[273]
> I have fame here in Tubondo,
> (I) Mwindo,
> Tubondo (with) seven meeting places,
> With seven entrances.
> He who will go beyond what Mwindo has said,
> He will die (from) seven lightnings—
> And one more in addition![274]

---

270. *įraį/the will*: before dying, fathers, headmen, chiefs, and other officials orally make their will known. The will bears on succession to office more than on inheritance of goods; it also sets forth various taboos and injunctions. There are strong magicoreligious sanctions against nonobservance of the will.

271. *Kįrų́ká-Mbų́ra . . . . Kákíríá/Kiruka-Mbura . . . who makes the trees fall*: Kákíríá (who makes . . . fall) has been translated in conjunction with Kįrų́ká. It is perfectly possible, however, that two different persons are designated here: first, the divinity of lightning (Nkuba) under the epithet Kįrų́ká-Mbų́ra; second, Mwindo himself under the epithet Kákíríá, "the little one who makes the trees fall in the forest."

272. *Rukombora nkombóre réro/Substitute, replace me now!*: an exclamation inserted by the narrator; he is tired and now desires a replacement. The substantive and verb used are Nyangaized forms of the Swahili verb *kukomboa* (to redeem, to deliver).

273. *Iyobora*: lit., opener; an epithet for the divinity of lightning, another epithet is *Mírábyo* (flashes).

274. *ná nįmá nti ÿawįtómo/and one more in addition*: wįtómo stands for the part the person in charge of distributing goods is allowed to set aside for himself before the actual distribution takes place; it is a supplement to which he is entitled because of his special duties. The expression is used here to insist that the individual who transgresses Mwindo's injunctions will certainly die.

The counselors howled, saying
That what has been said will be resaid.
And the common man is incapable of judgment;
Even Shemumbo is incapable of judgment.[275]
Absentminded ones, be never again distracted.
And an old man, he too is incapable of judgment.
It is the great chief who sustains the common man,
And it is the chief's wives who sustain the people.[276]
The words of the *nkebe*-dance are (of) wisdom.[277]
Nyamumbo howled, saying:
"If you arrive at Shemwindo's,
What Shemwindo will say
Will be the announcement of something living.[278]
If Shemwindo says a word,
He will die (from) seven lightnings.
We shall lack the one who will utter a word,
"We."
Nyamwindo howled saying:
"My son has suffered much.
Slander in this village is outrageous.
Someone's mother-in-law
Allows herself to criticize (that) someone;
And even someone's father-in-law
Allows himself to criticize (that) someone.
A giant of a young man
Laughs at the young woman's.[279]

275. *Is incapable of judgment*: i.e., has not the authority or the capacity to judge, to render a verdict.

276. *muhangá/great chief: stronger than mwami* (chief); refers to a chief who has great fame and who rules over more people than other chiefs.

277. *nkebe-dance*: the short songs used in this common Nyanga dance are mostly proverbs, *mishúma* (more commonly *mishų́mo*)/*words . . . of wisdom*: lit., proverbs, maxims, apothegms.

278. *mwasį́ wakárí-ho . . ./the announcement of something living . . .*: these verses can only be understood in the following way: according to Nyamumbo (Mwindo's mother) the words and decisions of her husband, Shemwindo, are good and adequate; according to Mwindo, his father's deeds are evil; Shemwindo must abstain from making decisions, lest he cause his own destruction.

279. *wamánubá/has suffered*: lit., has suffered from the heat. *Katéré kakúno kásuma/ Slander in this village is outrageous*: this and the following four verses are extremely terse statements. Literally they could be translated as follows:

A Mubuya (today) rainmaker
Formerly did not like to remove dew—
Remover of oil dew.
In Ihimbi, in our country, it is fine;
From it came out an epic.[280]
There lived a divinator.
Stump of the path of the river (trail)
Tears up the clothing of the elegant woman."

When Nkuba was returning with Mwindo, he went on slowly descending with him; he went and let him down in the very middle of the village place of Tubondo. When his father Shemwindo saw his son being brought back by Nkuba, he gave Nkuba a reward of a maiden who was dressed with a bracelet of copper of Nkuba; they also gave him the prescribed white fowl.[281] It is there that originated the custom of rendering cult to Nkuba; from then on they always dedicated to him a maiden and her copper ring.[282] After Nkuba had received (his) gift, he returned to his domain in the sky.

After Mwindo had taken rest, he assembled all his people. They arrived. He told them: "I, Mwindo, the Little-one-just-born-he-

---

Slander of this side is tough:
For a man's mother in law
Slanders (that) man;
And even a man's father-in-law
Slanders (that) man.

Cáseá cámwána múkari/Laughs at the young woman's: the implication is that he makes fun of the young woman's words or problems or "thing" (i.e., sex).

280. *A Mubuya rainmaker*: the narrator refers specifically to a person of the Babuya whom he has known. *In Ihimbi*: the narrator boasts that Ihimbi, the region where he was born and lived, is the cradle of the epic he is relating.

281. *a bracelet of copper of Nkuba*: Nyanga women, who are dedicated to the divinity of lightning, wear this bracelet as one of the distinctive emblems of the cult, *nénkókó yényangé/and the prescribed white fowl*: "prescribed" in our translation is justified by the augmen é-.

282. As in a few other instances, the epic attempts here to account for the origin of particular Nyanga customs. A large number of Nyanga women are dedicated to the divinities of lightning, good fortune, and so on; for many, the implication is that they are married to the spirit and cannot be normally married. These women live in prolonged union with married or unmarried men who have no rights to their children. These children belong to their mother's (i.e., the spirit wife's) descent group.

walked, performer of many wonderful things, I tell you the news from the place from where I have come in the sky. When I arrived in the sky, I met with Rain and Moon and Sun and Kubikubi-Star and Lightning. These five person-ages forbade me to kill the animals of the forest and of the village, and all the little animals of the forest, of the rivers, and of the village, saying that the day I would dare to touch a thing in order to kill it, that day (the fire) would be extinguished; then Nkuba would come to take me without my saying farewell to my people, that then the return was lost forever." He also told them: "I have seen in the sky things unseen of which I could not divulge." When they had finished listening to Mwindo's words, those who were there dispersed. Shemwindo's and Nyamwindo's many hairs went say "high as that" as the long hairs of an *mpaca*-ghost; and in Tubondo the drums had not sounded anymore; the rooster had not crowed any more.[283] On the day that Mwindo appeared there, his father's and his mother's long hairs were shaved, and the roosters crowed, and that day (all) the drums were being beaten all around.[284]

When Mwindo was in his village, his fame grew and stretched widely. He passed laws to all his people, saying:

> May you grow many foods and many crops.
> May you live in good houses; may you moreover live in a beautiful village.
> Don't quarrel with one another.
> Don't pursue another's spouse.
> Don't mock the invalid passing in the village.
> And he who seduces another's wife will be killed!
> Accept the chief; fear him; may he also fear you.
> May you agree with one another, all together; no enmity in the land nor too much hate.
> May you bring forth tall and short children; in so doing you will bring them forth for the chief.[285]

283. *mpacá/ghost*: specter of the forest; occurs in many Nyanga tales; has much hair, very long nails, and is always fomenting evil plans.

284. *ékwantsí ně̌kwiyo/all around*: lit., on earth and in the sky.

285. *wátanga/stretched widely*: lit., had many ramifications, like the branches of a tree, *washámbárá/he who seduces*: lit., to talk privately with. . . . *băna bare-bare na bihį-bíhį/tall and short children*: i.e., children of all kinds.

After Mwindo had spoken like that, he went from then on to remain always in his village. He had much fame, and his father and his mother, and his wives and his people! His great fame went through his country; it spread into other countries, and other people from other countries came to pay allegiance to him.

Among children there are none bad; whether he be disabled, or whether he not be disabled, he must not be rejected. So then there is nothing bad in what God has given to man.

Heroism be hailed! But excessive callousness either pushes a man into a great crime or brings him a great one, which (normally) he would not have experienced. So, whosoever in a country is not advised will one day carry excrements—and to experience that is terrible.

Mutual agreement brings about kinship solidarity; the one who will save his companion is unknown; it is like the chief and his subordinates. So, the world is but made of mutual aid. So, then, may the chief safeguard (his) subordinates and the subordinates safeguard the chief. Kingship is the stamping (of feet); it is the tremor of people.

Even if a man becomes a hero (so as) to surpass the others, he will not fail one day to encounter someone else who could crush him, who could turn against him what he was looking for.[286]

286. These four statements contain the narrator's explanation or his interpretation of the moral of the epic. The Nyanga traditionally give explanations in a very terse style for the stories they narrate, *n'erísúma rátáá katí, but excessive callousness*: the idea of excess is rendered in Nyanga by the expression *rátáá katí*, lit., which throws away (or which buries) the branch/tree/stick. There are two possible ways to interpret the connection between the terms. When clearing the forest for cultivation, the Nyanga do not put much care into the cleaning operation: after the banana stipes have been planted, trees are cut down and left on the spot without burning, thus giving the banana grove the appearance of neglect and negligence. To carefully remove branches, and so on, would indeed be a form of excess and might be considered to be inspired by some evil plans. The expression may also be related to current ideas about the secret activities of sorcerers. The verb *itáa* means to throw away, but also to bury. Sorcerers are said to bury certain vegetal or other materials in order to cause evil. Excess and evil, toughness and disregard for established patterns of behavior are all evoked by this expression, *buma-kjma/kinship solidarity*: lit., the state of being one; one of the terms that currently designates kinsmen. *Kafékúmbúka kúrjkangá ntí maramyana hó/So, the world is but made of mutual aid*: lit., so the world is seated being mutual saving (healing). *Kingship is the stamping (of feet)* . . .: that is, there is no chief without people and a chief can only have a multitude of people if he is a generous protector of them. *muraj ráréngá íréngá bjné/a hero (so as) to surpass the others*: lit., a hero, in a way that surpasses to surpass the com

panions (the congeners, the age-mates), *wámushée kísondángé we/who could turn against him what he was looking for*: lit., who could show him the thing that he is looking for. The Nyanga have a profound dislike for boasting and megalomania. For this reason they dislike making subjective evaluations of the relative moral or physical qualities of specific individuals. In most of the epic, the hero Mwindo behaves like an arrogant boaster, blindly believing in his own power. For the auditors, the hero's attitude caused reactions of uneasiness and sarcasm. Yet, there was an excuse for the hero as long as he was the victim of his father's unjust decisions and actions. The personality of the hero would ultimately have been unacceptable to the Nyanga if a moment of crisis and restraint had not come into his life. The moment came, after Mwindo had found his father, when the lightning spirit acting as a *deus ex machina* carried him away to the realm of Rain, Moon, Sun, Star to be castigated by them. The hero's incapacity to be successful in all circumstances made him acceptable to the Nyanga. In a great many of their stories, the Nyanga manifest strong fatalism and skepticism; even the sacred chiefs are limited in power and intelligence by superior beings, sometimes by the creator god himself. The statement, then, conceived as one of the morals of the epic, is in its wording both euphemistic and elliptical. The narrator means to say that there does not exist an individual so great as to surpass all others; even the Nyanga hero is not immune, but is subject to limitations set by superior forces and by immanent justice. Grammatically, the statement is to be considered as part of a cryptic dialogue between two individuals: one provoking the other and the other saying: "Beware, you look for trouble, and trouble you will get!"

INDEX

Aardvark, 13, 21, 26–27 *passim*, 99 and n. 190, 100 n. 193. *See also* Munundu; Ntumba

Ablution ceremonies, 61 n. 103, 80 n. 154

Adze, 23, 54 and n. 68, 82. *See also* Mwindo, magical possessions of

Affinal relationships, 5, 13, 15, 39 n. 1, 42 nn. 16 and 19, 47, 48 n. 40, 66 n. 110, 124 n. 247, 137 and n. 279. *See also* Marriage

Agnatic relatives, 3, 4, 11

Agriculture, 2–3, 33, 77, 84, 93 and n. 181, 94 and n. 183, 97, 105 n. 206, 113 n. 220, 114, 140–141 n. 286. *See also* Banana; Economy; Technology

Ancestors, 4, 5, 9

Animals, 17, 18, 21, 25, 30, 80, 85, 115 n. 226, 121 n. 239, 125 n. 251, 136, aquatic, 63; domestic, 115 n. 226; dramatis personae, 9, 13, 20; of the forest, 134, 139; little, of the forest, 139; of the river, 139; sacred, 9, 99 n. 190; of the village, 134, 139. *See also* Aardvark; Antelope; Bats; Birds; Boar, wild; Buffalo; Bush baby; Cattle; Chimpanzee; Dogs; Elephant; Fish; Genet; Goats; Gorilla; Hedgehog; Insects; Kasengeri;

Kihuká; Leopard; Monkey; *Muhangu*-animal; Otter; Pig; Sheep; Snail; Snake; Squirrel, flying; Turtle

Anointment, 125 and n. 249

Antelope, 5, 9, 11, 21; bongo, 43 and n. 18; Duiker, 9; *mukaka*, 55 and n. 78

Aphorisms, 6

Apostrophe, meaning of, 34

Apothegms, 137 n. 277

Armlets, 13, 123 nn. 242 and 243

Arrows, 60, 100 n. 193, 112 n. 218, 123

Art, plastic, 5

Ashes, 91, 93 and n. 179

Assembly, 43, 45, 47; description of mass, 116–125

Associations, 5, 76 n. 144, 132 n. 264. See also *Bwami*; Mukuki

Atmosphere, 20

Attendants, 47

Audience, vi, 7, 12

Aunt, paternal, 4, 11, 18–20, 21–29 *passim*, 31, 32, 47n.39, 54 n. 69, 58 n. 90, 58 n. 91, 62, 65–66, 70, 75 n. 140, 78, 80, 84–91 *passim*, 95–96 *passim*, 102–108 *passim*, 120, 124. *See also* Iyangura

Axe, 21, 22, 25, 69, 85, 94, 97, 98, 117

Tail: animal, 67 n. 115, 136; antelope, 21, 54 n. 67, 135 n. 269; boar, wild, 135 n. 269; buffalo, 21, 54 n. 67; elephant, 135 n. 269

Tales, 2, 5, 9, 19, 46 n. 32, 55 n. 76, 58 n. 90, 63 n. 105, 68 n. 120, 68–69 nn. 121 and 123, 71 n. 131, 78 n. 150, 89 n. 167, 92 n. 174, 96 n. 186, 126 n. 253

Taro leaves, 48

Technology, 2–3, 5, 33, 39, 41 n. 2, 44 n. 23, 53 n. 66, 75 n. 141, 76, 80–84, 93 and n. 181, 94–95, 101 n. 194, 114, 130 n. 261. *See also* Banana; Economy; Material culture

Telepathic bond, 96 n. 186

Thunder, 80

Tiri-Asa, 1, 2

Tobacco, 82

Tone, 7, 34, 59 n. 93, 79 n. 153, 103 n. 200, 106 n. 209

Torches, 60

Toro, 1. *See also* Uganda

Transcription, system of, 34–35

Translation, problems of, viii, 35–36, 106 nn. 208 and 209

Trap, 107 n. 210

Trapping, 2, 5, 9, 14, 39 n. 2, 67 n. 112, 82, 114, 126, 133, 134 n. 266. *See also* Economy

Trees, 115 n. 225, 136 and n. 271; ficus, 72; isea, 104; mango, 94; ntongi, 69; ntsembe (ntsémbe), 44 and n. 22; raphia, 19, 39 n. 2, 44, 54 n. 69, 84, 86 n. 162, 123 n. 242, 129 and n. 260, 132 n. 263, 133

"True stories," 9

Tube, reed, 11

Tubi, Stephano, v, vii, viii

Tubondo, 19–20, 21, 23, 25, 28, 39 and n. 2, 42, 46, 49, 57, 58, 61, 75, 78–82, 83–90, 95, 96, 101, 104, 107, 108, 109, 112–116 118, 119, 120, 124, 124, 126, 128, 129 n. 260, 130, 132, 135–139. *See also* Village

Turtle, 50 n. 51

Twa, 2. *See also* Baremba; *Batwá*; Pygmies

Twins, 40 n. 3

Uganda, 11, 61 n. 46

Ukanga, 29

Ukaru-powder, 137

Uncles: maternal, 26, 29, 30, 36–37, 39, 40, 44, 54 and n. 15, 79–80 n. 110, 92, 94, 98, 99, 102–103, 124–125, 128, 138 n. 246; paternal, 13. *See also* Baniyana; Bats

Underworld, 14, 30, 31, 37, 73 n. 97

University of Delaware, 7

Upstream, 59 n. 33, 71 n. 89, 75 and n. 103, 77

Utebe-stool, 60, 61, 125

Valuables, 57

Values, 6, 16, 17, 20, 24, 28–30, 32, 33, 43–45 *passim*, 76 n. 105, 100 n. 162, 120 n. 207, 129, 133, 135, 139, 148–149, 154–155 n. 286. *See also* Generosity; Hospitality

Van den Berghe, Louis, 7

Vegetables, 34; *isusa*, 63; *mususa*, 91 and n. 148

Village, 14, 31, 36, 40–42, 51 and n. 2, 53, 56, 58 n. 29, 59 n. 33, 69 and nn. 79 and 90, 73 n. 97, 110, 117 n. 201, 124, 125 and n. 216, 127, 128 and n. 223, 129, 142, 143 n. 257, 148, 149 n. 268, 154. See also *Kumbúka*; Tubondo

Volcanoes, 14

Vowels, symbols for, 45

Walilake, 11, 51 n. 2

Water, 14, 15, 34, 36

Water serpent, 14, 20, 24, 31–34 *passim*, 53. *See also* Mukiti; Musoka

Weirs, 121 n. 210

Whooping, 23, 143, 144 n. 210

Wiki- (*Wikí-*) game, 29, 39, 118, 126 and n. 218; seeds, 119

Will, 150 and n. 270. *See also* Inheritance

Wind, 14